Leaving Alva
Leaving Alva
Leaving Alva
Leaving Alva

VICTORIA LIPMAN

T0106627

SIMON & SCHUSTER

SIMON & SCHUSTER
Rockefeller Center
1230 Avenue of the Americas
New York, NY 10020

Designed by Deirdre C. Amthor

Manufactured in the United States of America

10 9 8 7 6 5 4 3 2 1

Library of Congress Cataloging-in-Publication Data
Lipman, Victoria.
Leaving Alva / Victoria Lipman.
p.   cm.
I. Title.
PS3562.I5774L4   1998
813'.54—dc21   97-23021 CIP
ISBN 978-1-4391-8326-7

Acknowledgments

I would like to thank my agent, Charlotte Sheedy; my editor, Chuck Adams; Robley Wilson who published my first short story; and Martha Moutray who provided encouragement and support.

To Bill, Ariana and Alida

Chapter One

I had been feeling restless for months, a kind of palsy of the mind, and only the thought of leaving town on a night bus calmed me.

Indian summer had come and gone. The sky had taken on the bruised color of early winter. I had tried everything: yoga, tai chi, biofeedback, subliminal messages. I drove around in Alva's car, cutting a big swath around the bus station which centered the town like some gaseous sun. I prayed, chanted my mantra, gave myself self-help talks, sometimes in public places in a loud voice, just to make sure that I was listening. It didn't matter whether I told myself that I was a bad person and ought to be ashamed or that I was a good person and could resist this temptation or simply an OK person who needed acceptance—none of it mattered. More than anything I wanted to get the hell out of that town and out of a life that shrink-wrapped me like a pork chop on a pink plastic tray.

I'd be leaving a job. A no-benefits job with a boss who liked to get me in the darkened storage room and stick his tongue in my mouth. Mostly I just pushed him away, told him he had bad breath or his wife was on the phone.

"You know you like it." He said this while pressing his bony self against me. My back flattened up against a file cabinet and the handle gouged into my back.

"Woody, this is not right," I told him as I tried to drill my fist into his chest.

"Just one little kiss." Woody's idea of one little kiss was letting his tongue go so far down my throat that my tonsils could wear it as a muffler. If he had the time, he would count my teeth with his tongue. I could feel the pens in his shirt pocket pressing into my left breast, his hands around my waist but on the move. I couldn't take it anymore. I kneed him in the crotch. That was Friday, right before quitting time. Maybe I didn't have a job anymore.

The only part of the job that I liked was wearing a hard hat when I went into the warehouse to check on the orders. There I talked to the ladies in packing, hired mostly for the size of their biceps and their willingness to work for less money than men. They told me dirty jokes. I laughed a lot.

I've got a husband too.

My husband, Alva Edward Herson, is a fine enough man if breathing steady is a big factor. Actually, he is better than that. His main problem is that he is so boring. I could predict exactly what he would do and how he would do it. His habits were so set that hunting him wouldn't be any challenge. Every day, he had two Fig Newtons in his lunch and hot cocoa at 9:30 P.M. right before the news, then off to bed at ten. It took him exactly twelve minutes to get up and come to breakfast, and the toothbrush and shaving cream were always left in the same spot. He's got about ten expressions that cover most any occasion he's likely to encounter—things like "no fooling" and "I can believe that" and "you don't say." So the man is predictable and no conversationalist, can you leave a man for that? No, I couldn't. None of my selves could, not even the bad you-ought-to-be-ashamed-of-yourself self could.

But he watched me all the time.

Sometimes I felt like a television set, the way he looked at me as if taking his eyes off me for one second would make things go all goofy in the world. As if I were cueing him which way to turn, as if the big silver jet had no one on board and I were down there with my red light waving him into port. It was like that all the time, and if he wasn't watching me, he watched television. Didn't matter so much what was on, as long as his eyes were occupied. Maybe the problem was anxious eyes. Was that a strong enough case for leaving a man?

I left Alva a note. I propped it up against the sugar bowl on the kitchen table.

You're a good husband Alva, but good isn't enough. Your goodness is only the kind that means you have no badness. You're at the wall but you've never been over. I've renewed your subscription to the TV Guide *for two more years so I could get the lower rate. If you move, make sure you notify them of your change of address.*

I'll mail you power of attorney so you can get the divorce papers started. I didn't take anything that didn't belong to me. My half of the savings and my clothes. Tell your children the next time you get them, that I think they're great kids.

You deserve better than me.

Chloe

I stood in front of the Destination Map of the World According to Greyhound, with my bags wedged between my feet. I ruled out all the places where it snowed, all the places I couldn't afford the fare, everything with a green-headed pin stuck on it, states that had a North and a South in their names, but mostly I just didn't want to be cold again. All my life I had felt cold, probably from a childhood spent in cheap, underheated motel rooms with blankets thinner than the gruel in an orphanage. I drew an imaginary snow line across the map and settled on Phoenix, Arizona.

Waiting in line to buy my ticket as I pushed my suitcases with my feet, things began to sink in. This wasn't one of my dreams that left me feeling confused about what was real and what wasn't. I was in the bus station. I had left Alva. I wasn't going to be waking up and making breakfast and moving like a robot through the day.

The line moved slowly. Didn't anybody know where they were going? What was so hard about saying "give me a one-way ticket to Phoenix, Arizona" or "give me a two-way ticket to Boise, Idaho"? It's not like you had to pick out your seat right now, front or middle or back, window or aisle. They don't feed you on buses or ask you if you want headphones or a pillow or a magazine. I hoped they didn't allow smoking on buses anymore.

"A one-way ticket to Phoenix, Arizona, please."

The ticket agent barely glanced at me as he punched in my destination and my ticket spat out. "That will be forty-nine dollars." I wanted him to look up, to see me. I wanted to see my reflection in his glasses. He pushed my change back through the grate. "Enjoy your trip." He spoke to my back as I turned away.

I had two hours before my bus left, so I bought a soda and sat down to think about my future. I suppose some women might have cried by now but I wasn't like that. I never let myself cry right when something happened. Crying clouds the mind just when you need to be at your clearest. My tears sneak up on me during movies and the sad parts of books. Then I blame it all on what I'm seeing on the screen or reading, without having to admit that I have within me my own private well of sadness.

I had about a thousand dollars on me and a silver dollar that I found while sweeping out the cellar at Alva's house one early spring day. That day under a telephone spool I'd also found a nest of newborn mice, tiny and translucent with the slightest tinge of pink. I put the nest back where I found it after I had swept out the place. Rodent control wasn't in my job description. I liked Alva best when I was doing something, earning my keep, but I drew the line at massacring mice.

I finished my soda and started walking around the perimeter of my seat with the bags stationed in front. I stayed close enough to my bags so that if anyone tried to steal one, I could grab the culprit. It was like being on a tether, walking around with my eyes shifting back to my bags, then to the flower cart parked to the left of me, the vendor figuring his take for the day, rolling back the bills and counting with his mouth open.

The shoeshine man was as black as the polish he spread on the shoes of the man in the chair, who did his best to look around and pretend that another man wasn't at his feet polishing his shoes. The shoeshine man polished and slapped his rag at the shoe, moving his body as if to some song playing in his head. When he was done, he looked up at the man whose shoes he had polished, his white teeth in sharp contrast to his smooth dark skin covered with a fine sheen of light sweat. "You's done, sir. They look mighty fine." The man stepped down from the shoeshine throne and handed three bucks to the black man without so much as a thank-you or even a glance. The shoeshine man took the money and nodded. It didn't seem to matter much to him that his customer had acted as if he were invisible, though I'm sure it did. I think being invisible is one of the most painful things in this world.

I sat down. The molded plastic seat felt cold. I kept checking my watch against the giant clock on the wall. My life seemed to have slid into slow motion. I closed my eyes. Through my feet I could feel the diesel sound of the buses as they rolled into the tunnel underneath me. I snapped my eyes open to a thump. To my left the evening papers had landed, baled with string. The newsstand man rolled his cigar to the corner of his mouth and pouched his face in disgust at the retreating back of the paperboy. He dragged the papers, like a dead body, behind the counter.

I took a deep breath. Cigarettes, the sweetish odor of a pipe, diesel fumes seeping up through the ventilation system, that ashy street smell that you can taste in your mouth, carried on the clothes of the incoming passengers. I like to catalogue smells. It puts me in the moment, takes me out of my head and puts me in the same place as my body. I think of my body sometimes as being separate from me. My body as a method of locomotion, my body as a large container for my head, my body as a companion to my mind, my body as a kind of trusty to the warden of my mind. I'm really into this mind/body thing.

"Bus 279 departing for Phoenix, Arizona, leaving from gate

number eighteen at four P.M., is now boarding." The announcement cut right into my thinking and with great relief I picked up my suitcase and followed the sign to gates one through twenty-five. I passed gates for Dubuque, St. Louis, Las Vegas, and Kansas City, where buses stood like silent silver hounds. The rest of the parking spaces were empty with only stains on the pavement to mark the spot. I didn't worry about Alva coming after me. He never came home before six o'clock.

The porter loaded luggage into the underbelly of the bus after checking the ticket of each passenger. I handed both of my suitcases over and he glanced at my ticket and nodded. I walked to the front of the bus, used the handrail to pull myself up the steps, and stood for just a second surveying the seats available.

I counted down eighteen rows and decided that I belonged on the left-hand side of the bus. I put my backpack on the window seat hoping that people would think that I was saving it for someone else. Window seats are good for sightseeing and for reading and following the stripe along the night road until you fall asleep.

I settled into the vinyl seat and watched the passengers enter the bus and scope things out. A woman on the far side of fifty marched down the aisle holding her purse in front of her like a shield. She went straight to the back and took the last seat on the left-hand side.

Not everybody takes a bus, you know. Only certain people will take buses. Mostly people without a car or the cash to fly, or those afraid of falling off a train or having a plane fall out of the sky. I watched them get on one by one. Each had a story and I liked giving them little opening lines. A straggly haired blonde girl with coal black roots and a top that wouldn't cover a bra if she were wearing one and snug blue jeans strode down the aisle like she had done this a hundred times before. She wasn't at all excited. She had her seat picked out before she was born—that seat being the one right in front of me. She bumped into it and slid down until I could see only a few strands of hair.

A couple got on—you know the kind, mated for life, already done fifty years together, each knows everything about the other, and when one dies, the other will die within six months. He held her arm gently and guided her down the aisle. She smiled like they're taking the grand tour and he whispered in her ear every step of the way. I wanted to believe in them, but that came hard to me. Maybe they were what they seemed. But maybe he's plotted her death while she lies asleep and she's thought of giving him a gentle shove at the head of the stairs. Believing in the Easter Bunny comes easier to me than having faith in the feelings of others. They sat across from me.

Finally the bus was loaded. I found myself gussetted in by people while whole pockets of the bus remained empty. What was I? A magnet? The driver stood up front. "We'll be departing in five minutes. I'll be giving the final call. This bus is headed for Phoenix, Arizona, with stops at . . ." He rattled off the names of cities without taking a breath. Then he got off and went over to the phone reserved for employees and spoke in short sentences to someone at the other end. An announcement came over the loudspeaker. This last call brought a gaggle of latecomers, mostly male, and the last two on were guys in their twenties wearing long ponytails, each sporting a diamond stud in his left ear.

At first everyone ignored everyone else, kind of like some travelers' courtesy, but those in it for the long haul to Phoenix would probably want to talk.

About twenty minutes into the trip, the old guy leaned over and asked me the time. I told him. Then fifteen minutes later, he turned sideways in his seat and asked me if I'd like a stick of gum and don't the air in these buses get mighty old? I agreed, took the gum, and he had all the encouragement he was going to need. "The missus and I are going to visit one of our kids. We got six, you know. All turned out OK except for Zeke and he's had a hard time of it."

I nodded. I knew that was all I had to do.

"We never quite figured out what was wrong with Zeke." He reached over with his mottled grayish-looking hand covered in a mat of furry white hair and grabbed his wife's pudgy fingers. "We thought maybe something went wrong at the hospital. Something they didn't tell us about. Like maybe they was giving him a bath and he slipped and fell on the floor. They got concrete floors there, you know. Zeke was born in a hospital. Only one of ours who was, we'd moved in off the farm, and the only one who's had such troubles."

His fingers picked at the creases in his pants. He looked as if he had forgotten where he was, what he was going to say next. I prompted him. "What troubles has he had?"

The old guy was off. The story of Zeke was about to be told again and I think in some sense this story of Zeke was a kind of morality tale for the old man. He knew there was a message in there somewhere but he hadn't yet figured out what the message was, though plenty of people had offered up explanations.

"Zeke was always a sweet baby but sometimes he'd just fly into these screaming fits when he'd curl up his little fists and twist his little body side to side and just scream until his face turned so red we thought he'd just blow up. We tried everything from holding him real tight to throwing ice water on him; we even prayed but nothing helped. He didn't get much better as he got older but he changed. He'd still scream but then he started banging his head against the wall and wetting himself even when he was much too old for that.

"Then when he turned twelve, he stopped all that and got real quiet. He'd sit for hours doing nothing and we was grateful for that but still he wasn't a regular boy."

The old guy paused. "My name is Cyrus and my missus is Sadie." He put his hand across the aisle and I shook it, surprised at how much strength it still had.

"I'm Chloe."

"Pleased to meet you. Now after Zeke got to be a teenager he started acting even funnier but he was still quiet. He'd sit there for hours. Sometimes he'd just start laughing out loud and pointing to the walls like there was something to see but we just saw walls. He was the youngest and of course the rest of the kids just closed in around him and kept an eye out. I don't think Zeke was ever alone much after that. He'd pretty much do what the other kids told him to."

"What's Zeke up to nowadays?"

"He's a janitor at the state institution for the insane. Lives with his sister Jennie. Her husband passed, leaving her with three kids. Zeke ain't much help with the kids but he gives her most of his check every week and helps out around the house. Jennie's going to night school and Zeke stays with the young'n's."

I figured this story to be winding down. Soon I could pull a book out of my backpack and do a little reading. "Sounds like Zeke is doing OK," I said.

Cyrus heaved a big sigh. "Townfolks almost run him out of town last summer."

"Why?"

"A little girl turned up missing. They found her body in the woods all mashed up but her mama still knew it was her."

I felt the chill of the processed air in the bus. I didn't say anything. Sadie, who had been staring out the window the whole time the old man told his story, swung her head in my direction. A twitch made her right cheek dance.

"Folks around there think Zeke's crazy. They say he ought not to be working at the institution, he ought to be in the institution."

"He does this pointing and laughing stuff in front of other people?" I figured even crazy people must know enough to hide their craziness some of the time.

"Well, not on purpose." The old man's voice rose up in defense of his crazy son. The way he'd been telling this story until now, you would think he'd read it in the newspaper. "We stuck by him."

I asked, being the forthright sort and possessing a degree of curiosity, "You think he did it?"

The old man waited so long before answering I thought he hadn't heard me and I'd have to ask again. "I don't know," he finally answered and sank back into his seat, leaving a space between us bigger than the Grand Canyon.

What would it be like to live with a person you loved and not know whether that person had killed someone? Not just killed someone, like in vehicular homicide or war, but bludgeoned a child to death? I mean, just saying he didn't know meant he thought it was possible that Zeke was guilty. Did he look at Zeke funny after the girl was found? Did he look at him like maybe he didn't know him? What if someone else died? Would that be the old guy's fault? I couldn't live with Alva and he was just boring. I guess if I even remotely suspected Alva of murder, anyone's murder, I'd have left sooner.

I couldn't let things rest. I moved closer to Cyrus, my knees almost touching his in the aisle. "What did the people in town do?"

The old man spoke slowly, as if I were reeling him in from a long distance. "Well, the police came around but Zeke couldn't say for sure where he had been all the time since the girl had disappeared, except for being at work. They had two of them doctors over at the hospital talk to him. One said he wouldn't hurt a fly; the other wasn't so sure. There was no real proof so no charges were ever brought. Some windows got broke at Jennie's and her tires slashed and some ugly phone calls. Then things died down. But every mother in town tells her kids to stay away from Zeke and even Jennie don't rest easy when he's with the kids alone. Not that she believes for a minute that Zeke could do anything like that."

"How's Zeke taking all this?" I asked.

"Not good at all. It hurts him that children won't come near him except for a few boys who tease him and offer him their little sisters."

"Kids really do that?"

Cyrus explained, "They don't mean it, not really. They're just boys trying to prove they're not just boys."

The conversation seemed to suck the power of speech right out of the old man. He turned away from me and never spoke to me for the rest of the trip. His wife returned to her vigil at the window and when I tried to catch her eye later in the trip, she looked at me as if I were some foreign tourist she just couldn't understand.

After Cyrus's story I shifted to my window seat and pulled my paperback out of the backpack. The catalogue of Alva's faults and bad habits that I had compiled over our years together seemed mean-spirited and trivial compared to Cyrus's trial with Zeke. I felt guilt rising up like bile in my throat. I couldn't stick with a man who left his underwear scattered about the floor like a bread trail, while old Cyrus hung in there with a suspected child killer. I could feel myself losing color, turning gray with guilt, my energy bubbling out of me like a slow air leak. I snapped the spine on my book. The crack brought me back to the real world. It wasn't the same thing, I told myself. I straightened my back and started to read.

Chapter Two

She left when the darkness came. They had been playing cards, all four of them, as twilight deepened its hold upon the backyard. I stood at the screen door looking for fireflies, listening: the clink of ice in the glasses, the steady sound of voices, the cards shuffled into disorder. I tried to pick out her voice. I always had to know where she was. I never knew what she might do.

Fireflies blinked into the night. Mothers called out for their children to come home. I opened the freezer door and rooted among the iced-up packages to find the Fudgsicle I had hidden in the back. I tore off the paper wrapper and rinsed off the ice under the faucet. The taste of the chocolate calmed me. My tongue worked the frozen bar first up one side and then down the other, a quick swipe off the top. Timing was important. Don't eat so fast that it's over too soon but not so slow that the 'sicle melts down your hand.

When I finished, I licked the wooden stick clean and put it in my pocket. Then I licked each finger until they weren't sticky anymore. I walked into the living room. The sofa was covered with unfolded laundry and stacks of magazines. There was still a small spot where I could fit on the end of the sofa. I climbed up there and curled up. Four long-necked beer bottles stood on the card table and cigarette smoke mushroomed about the table so that the people seemed to be inside the smoke. Mama wore a blue dress and her good necklace. I could smell her perfume from where I sat. My Sin—Daddy had bought her that for Christmas. The other woman was Shirley. She came around sometimes at night when Daddy was at work and brought her friends with her. Her friends were always men, always two men. They would all drink and talk, play cards, listen to music. If they decided to dance, Tom and I had to go to our rooms, and if the baby cried, no one paid any attention. I wasn't supposed to come out, but I cracked my door a little and peeked. After a while the music kept playing but nobody danced. Shirley and her friend would be sitting on the sofa real close and sometimes I guessed they lay down to rest. I don't know where Mama went, though I knew she was in the house. I could hear her laughing or saying "hush now" to Shirley's friend.

I asked Mama once why Shirley came over with her friends.

"Because I want them to. I need some fun. Just because I got three kids don't mean I'm dead yet."

"I'll play with you."

"It's not the same thing. Now go outside."

But tonight was different. I fell asleep on the sofa and woke up when the music clicked off. They were leaving, all four of them. Shirley and her friend were already out the door. I called out "Mama" but she didn't turn around. She followed Shirley out and a man pulled the front door shut. I looked around the room. They hadn't cleaned up. Mama always cleaned up, put the card table back in the hall closet and the folding chairs out in the garage. Then she'd open up all the windows and let the smoke out. After she washed up the glasses, she double-bagged the trash and went out to the can. She lifted out all the bags on top and then put the new bag on the bottom. Then she'd put vanilla extract in water and heat it up on the stove. She said it gave the house a "homey smell." Tom and I had been told never to tell Daddy that she had company when he was gone. Mama said he wouldn't understand. He was so much older than she was that sometimes she felt like he was her father. And having a father tell you what to do when you were a grown-up lady wasn't a very nice thing to have. And anyway she'd whip us if we told, and Daddy would whip us too for not telling him before. I was afraid of my father. I believed her.

Tom came into the living room. He was nine with yellow hair.

"She's gone. When's she coming back?"

He shrugged. "Daddy will be home soon."

"Who will take care of us?"

Tom said again that Daddy would be home soon.

"Who will feed us?"

He scowled. "Shut up, you big baby."

Tom didn't know how bad things were. I knew already that she wasn't coming back. A hole in my heart kept widening with every breath I took.

"Don't start that breathing stuff." He walked over to the card table and picked up a bottle of beer. He upended it into his mouth and puckered his face at the taste.

My breath wasn't going into me the way it should. I was starting to feel shaky.

Tom picked up another bottle and emptied it into his O-shaped mouth. "Cut that out or I'm going to my room and lock my door and then you'll be all alone and the bogeyman will come for you because I know that both the front and back door are unlocked. And I won't stop him."

I wrapped my arms around myself as if I were hugging someone and I held on tight. My breath slowed until I could barely hear the in and out whoosh, and my heart stopped pounding as I counted out one-two-three-four-five.

Tom looked over and smiled at me. "I'll lock the doors now."

The baby started to cry but Tom and I just sat on the sofa, he at one end perched on top of the laundry and me at the other as we waited for Daddy to come home.

Chapter Three

After several more hours of silence, the bus rolled into a rest stop and everyone got off. Before I left, I sized up the location of those empty pockets and decided to get a new seat.

The women formed a human chain in front of the washroom while the men seemed split between the men's room and a leg-stretcher walk. As I moved my way up the line, I checked out the concession stand but decided to hold on to my cash. The bathroom had that universal bathroom odor of dampness and unseen life-forms. I watched to see who didn't wash her hands. This whole bathroom thing was kind of like a ritual: the skirt straightening, the slip checking, pulling the lips back to look for lipstick stains. Everyone seemed conscious of the line waiting to get inside and the presence of the silver bus with PHOENIX, ARIZONA tattooed across its forehead in the parking lot. Nobody took too much time, as if some invisible game clock ticked away the minutes. Some women gave the mirror a meaningful gaze, like they were thanking it for showing them back to themselves and not surprising them with the reflection of another. A few barely looked, giving more attention to the scrubbing of their hands, front and back, between the fingers, washing twice with a good rinse in between. I got in the stall and out without touching anything except the toilet paper and then I imitated the hand washing but I didn't look in the mirror. I've never been one to look in the mirror much. I don't really know why.

I decided to walk around, and while making my third turn around the building I saw the two guys with diamond studs in their ears hiding behind some crates in a corner. They were sharing a cigarette and the one who was puffing on it hid the cigarette behind his back when I passed by. His cheeks ballooned with smoke that he held in, and he gave me a tight little smile. His friend just stared at me in a kind of ugly, slack-jawed way and held his hand out for what I figured was a joint. I tried to remember where they were sitting on the bus. Maybe I'd be the last one to get on. Men looked at me sometimes but I never looked back. I went past them and turned toward the front of the building. The passengers had clotted into little groups, talking and smiling, sharing destinations and complaints about the speed of the bus, praising the countryside and in general practicing what I like to think of as social lubrication. I have never been any good at that sort of thing.

The bus driver, whose name tag read STAN, called the all-aboard. I hung around the edge of the group until everyone, including the two men, had boarded. Stan looked at me but said nothing. I got on and with a quick glance headed toward one of the empty blocks of seats. I was pretty well pleased with myself and was thinking about maybe taking up two seats by flinging my legs across the next one when the blonde with the black roots got up out of her seat and moved toward me. She stared right at me. I looked out the window to the gas pumps and the concession stand where the lights had just gone on. I didn't want company. She sat down next to me. Didn't even ask if I minded. She just folded up those long skinny legs and sat down like some kind of puppet next to me. I kept looking out the window.

The doors hissed closed. The bus lurched into motion, picking up speed as we got back on the highway. Once out on the road, Stan seemed intent on pushing his way straight through to Phoenix. The countryside started to fly by with only a few markers like a red silo or a cluster of whitewashed buildings. Everything else was a blur of green and brown, fading into the oncoming darkness.

I looked out the window until my neck hurt. Then I peeked a quick one at the blonde. She sat reading a book. I tried to read the title without giving myself away. I couldn't, not the way she held the book, kind of closed up like she was reading down a narrow hallway. She paid no attention to me. Why did she sit next to me if she wasn't going to talk to me? I looked up to see the two men who had shared a cigarette turned around in their seats staring at her as if they also shared one pair of eyes. Now I knew why she sat next to me—I was to be the chaperone, another woman, the safety in numbers.

"I'm not going to have anything to do with those greaseballs," I announced.

She didn't look up from her book. "Me neither. I'm telling them you're my girlfriend."

I looked straight at her.

"As in girlfriend/boyfriend/date," she explained as if she were talking to the dim-witted.

I had made too much eye contact. If I hadn't looked at her, she wouldn't have sat next to me. I'm not the fastest thinker in the world. What was I supposed to say? I looked up again at the men. They stared. "We haven't spoken to each other before this," I said, my voice reasonable.

"I'll tell them we were having a little spat, a lovers' spat." She closed her book, a well-worn paperback, her hand flat on the cover.

"Can't you think of something else to tell them?" I thought about climbing over her and walking to the front of the bus to sit next to the old lady who talked at the bus driver and never noticed that he wasn't listening. I looked at her closely. Her skin had a porcelain whiteness.

"Like what?"

"How about you're engaged? You're married. You're on your way to the convent. You have the clap. You just had a hysterectomy."

"You're good, really good," she said.

The admiration in her voice filled me up. I'm sure I blushed. "What are you reading?"

She turned the book so that I could see the title. *Marya: A Life* by Joyce Carol Oates.

"You like to read?"

"I live to read. Books are my life. Words are my oxygen, sentences my very lifeblood."

"You make that up?"

"This very moment in time, birthed before your very ears."

"My name is Chloe, what's yours?"

"Zena."

"Z-E-N-A?"

"Yes, my mother worked in the circus and my dad was some kind of wage slave in town whenever they had a layover."

"What did your mother do in the circus?"

"She swallowed swords and walked across hot coals during show time. Kind of a side act for the main ring in which Babu the Great inserted objects larger than your head into his nose."

"No."

"Yes, truly, I never lie about certain things."

I didn't ask what those things were. "I don't have to kiss you, do I?"

The two guys conferred together, giving them the Siamese appearance of being joined at the forehead. They sat midway in the bus and the overhead lights made them look feral.

"You could just hold my hand and look deeply into my eyes." Zena reached for my hand. "Well, do you want those two sleazos coming back here?"

I held her hand and gave her what I hoped was a soulful gaze. She returned the look and was much better at it than I was. Then she leaned over and kissed me on the lips, pressing down just slightly, then pulling back. I haven't been kissed that way many times in my life. I guess you could say my life has not been filled with gentleness. I felt funny, but I wasn't sure what to call the feeling. I glanced up and the two guys looked at us in an entirely different way, as if we had just changed form in front of them, like in some kind of magic trick, when a handkerchief becomes a rabbit. I kind of liked it.

They turned toward each other, heads angled as if sharing a malted.

"Looks like there's only one of them." I wanted to share my insight with Zena. I wanted her to "get" it, to admire my cleverness.

She laughed. "They're sharing a brain. They're real slow thinkers. We'll be all right for a while."

"Then what?"

"Then one of them will appoint himself as official lesbian rescuer and do his best to turn me around."

I wanted to know if she really was a lesbian, but I was afraid to ask. I haven't any history of kissing or dating women, but I'm just as curious as the next person. I have heard stories about women doing it to each other with Coke bottles and cucumbers, but I don't believe everything I hear.

We started talking books. For a woman who looked like a cheap slut, she was quite bright. I have always taken the quiet way in dressing and speaking, mostly not wanting to draw attention to myself. This was clearly not Zena's way.

"John Steinbeck," I said.

Zena pronounced him a "genius." I nodded in agreement. She breathed, "Hemingway, another genius."

"A victim of testosterone overload," I said.

Zena frowned at me.

"Kate Chopin," I offered up, sure we would agree.

Zena bobbed her head. "Edna Pontellier in *The Awakening* would have done better to drown her bastard of a husband in the bathtub than walk into the sea herself."

I looked around. I felt as if everyone had been listening to us even though I knew better. They all sat facing forward, like an orderly regiment. The two sleazos had completely lost interest in us. Now headsets crowned their ratty heads, and their Jell-O necks swayed to the music.

We stopped talking, and for a few seconds the only sound came from the bus engine. It was as if we had all been flash frozen into silence. Then coughs, throat clearings, and gum snapping filled the void. Zena and I sat looking down at our hands, as if through books

we had told some secret about ourselves. I closed my eyes, willing
the bus into sound. As if on cue, the whole bus just lit up in the oncoming darkness with chuckles and easy flowing talk. It sounded
like everyone had known each other forever. Maybe it would have
happened without me. Maybe that kind of thing just happens
among strangers trapped inside a metal tube hurtling down the
highway. Maybe the approaching darkness brought it on, the way a
fire keeps away the jackals of night. I would like to take credit,
though. I wanted it to be my doing.

The dinner break came. We pulled into a graveled lot next to a
restaurant blazing brighter than a Christmas tree. It was so bright
that the glare hurt my eyes, gave me kind of an achy feeling down
deep in my sockets. Zena and I headed for the rest room first. I
watched Zena fuss with her hair, smooch her lips at herself in the
mirror, and pat her own rear end, all the while enjoying a side view
of herself in the water-spotted towel dispenser. I decided to comb
my hair. When people looked in mirrors, did they see what was really there? Or did they only see those beady eyes they hated or that
thin, scalp-chilling head of hair or those ears poised for takeoff?
Mirror, mirror on the wall, make me the fairest of them all. I never
had such hope. Not that I was troll ugly or anything like that. I
have regular features, dark hair, blue eyes, I'm about five-four.
Nothing particularly redemptive nor anything condemning. I'm just
there. I have all my body parts and they go together, nothing out of
proportion. I suppose I should be grateful. The truth is that when I
do look in the mirror, I sometimes don't recognize myself. A long
rubber band of time stretches out and I don't know who I'm looking at. My reflection startles as if I had come upon a complete
stranger while turning the corner of a hallway. And there we are,
nose to nose, our eyes riveting us together, hair standing up on my
neck, a fight-or-flight reaction. My being visible to others surprises
me as if I had no more form than windblown vapors.

By the time Zena finished in the bathroom, all the tables in the
dining room had been taken. Two more buses had pulled into the
lot and the room pulsed with movement. We both ordered a number
ten: hamburger, fries, and corn. We ate our meal leaning up against

one end of the counter that ran the full length of the restaurant. At each end of the counter was a door leading into the kitchen. Our door read OUT.

Cyrus and Sadie sat together silently, although for all I knew they were communicating telepathically. After all those years maybe you don't need words anymore. Everything had already been said.

The sleazos were nowhere to be seen. Probably out back sharing a joint.

While Zena and I ate our dinners, our driver circulated through the room telling each table that the bus to Phoenix left in twenty minutes. Zena helped herself to my fries and used my ketchup. I noticed every one that she took.

Dinner made me sleepy and, once settled in my seat, I rolled up my jacket and dozed off to the murmuring voices of my fellow passengers.

"Mashed potatoes tasted homemade."

"That broccoli was a bit rubbery."

"I wonder if the bus driver gets a kickback for making us eat in that dump."

"The best thing I could say about that meal is that I didn't have to make it, Walter."

"Yes, dear."

Although new passengers boarded sometime that night, I didn't see them. I woke up having to pee something fierce. Zena pressed up against me. I had one hell of a stiff neck. Dawn streaked across the sky, and when I shifted, Zena woke with a jump.

"It's OK," I mumbled, my mouth feeling gummy and my teeth grainy. "I hope we're stopping soon." Several people stood waiting to use the washroom on the bus. The bus began to slow and eased into the right lane and exited to a rest stop. This one looked a lot like the last one except that the soft, forgiving light of early morning gave the place a fairyland kind of glow. "Gotta go," I said to Zena between clenched teeth as I climbed over her to get to the aisle where I muttered a litany of excuse-me's while plowing my way forward. I walked to the john with my legs pressed tightly together. The relief of taking a pee when you're desperate is definitely a peak physical experience.

I met Zena on my way out. She muttered, "Black coffee." Being the first one off the bus had advantages. I picked up two cups of black coffee and snagged a metal table just in time to see the sun rise. I watched it come up cooler than it would go down, sort of humble, unsure of a welcome. I wished I had my toothbrush on me.

Zena came out looking wet. "Are there showers in there?" I asked. I hadn't noticed any, but until the caffeine kicks in, I'd make a lousy witness.

"No, I stuck my head under the sink." She took her coffee and finished it in three gulps. "The sleazos are gone. Got off in the middle of the night. Wasn't even a regular stop. They slipped the driver a ten and he let them off in the middle of nowhere."

"Says who?"

Zena said, "Some blue rinse with insomnia. I'm glad I'm never getting old."

"Right." The coffee was starting to clear the early morning fog out of my head.

"I won't. I can't. Bad genes."

I watched a jet leave a smoky hieroglyph in the sky.

"We got some new people. Think any of them play cards?" Zena scanned the parking lot.

"I don't know. Why?"

"Because I play cards, for money."

I asked, "Now how much money do people who ride buses have to spend?"

"More than you think. More than they should. Playing cards is not just a matter of budgetary restraints. People like to get lucky."

"They don't like to lose."

"No one who plays really thinks they're going to lose."

"But they do."

"Then they win again and their faith is restored."

"Is that how you make money?"

Zena said, "One of the ways."

I didn't ask what the other ways were.

•

Within twenty minutes Zena had found playing partners: two men in their fifties, with that beaten look that bad salesmen have. She sat in an aisle seat across from one of the men, and in the next row sat the other man. I finished out the foursome by sitting behind Zena also on the aisle. She kept winning, of course, but they kept smiling—mostly, I think, because of the way Zena scooped her shoulders in when she went to sweep up her winnings, giving them an unobstructed view of her breasts nicely nested in the fire-engine red tube top.

I could learn a lot from Zena. I was in high school before I finally stayed in one place long enough to get to know kids. But those kids were mostly townies, kids who never left the place except for the funerals of out-of-town relatives and then only if it couldn't be avoided. Like maybe there was a reading of the will to follow the burying or some ailing uncle who needed buttering up. Most of them seemed content to live that way. Thought the whole world was just balled up real tight in their little town. I couldn't see it myself. To them, I was like the lint in the dryer vent. I came from the clothes but nobody knew exactly where.

Every time Zena won, she would reach over and stroke the hands of the men in a soft, soothing way as if promising them better luck. I did that sometimes, touched myself, my face, my hands, my arms, with a hand that I pretended wasn't my own. It gave me comfort and I think I actually fooled myself sometimes. Fooled my body at least.

After a bit, the men pulled out their pocket linings and claimed poverty. Zena had cleaned them out. She owed them a drink, they said. First thing we get in Phoenix, I will, she promised, and then directed me to the back of the bus with a nod of her head.

"How much did you make?"

"Forty bucks, that's counting the two I won off you. You're a real wimpy bettor." She slid down into an empty seat.

I sat across from her. I asked, "You going to have a drink with them?"

"No way."

"I want to be just like you, Zena." My words surprised me. Me who usually knows what's coming out of my mouth about twenty seconds before it does.

"No, you don't. I could be an ax murderer for all you know."

"No, you couldn't."

"Maybe not. I don't have that much upper arm strength."

The grayer of the two men looked back at Zena. She smiled and moved her tongue over her lips like she was licking off something sweet.

"You like him?" Disgust veined my voice.

"He's just like everybody else, trying to get by."

"You do better than get by."

"You're seeing me on a good day."

I felt naked after what I'd said to Zena. But I did want to be just like her. In fact, part of me thought that maybe she *was* me, my missing half, the part of me that only hinted at existing but never came fully into sight. That shadowy self that never matched the person standing in the sun. Like there was a part of me that was quick and clever, but that part never got out the front door. I'd hear her voice sometimes softly and I'd think that I said my thought out loud, but I didn't. I figured myself to be smart, I could work things through. But I never ever felt quite like I was me. I have sorted through selves like clothes racked in the clearance section but never settled on any one. I have made efforts. But they were made not for the real me, they were made for the me that got squashed down while others were being the real them. So if I hadn't been squashed and flattened by my life, the real me would be out and maybe I would be just like Zena. Someone with a quick mouth, who knew where other people were weak and zoomed right in there and then out again with no complications. I wanted that for myself.

"How much money you got?" Zena turned to me with a small black wallet in the palm of her hand.

"I have three hundred and forty dollars." I truly had about nine hundred and fifty dollars but trust doesn't come easy to me.

"Ever been to Phoenix?"

"No."

"I grew up there. It's like a giant small town except you don't know your neighbors because they're always moving out and new ones are moving in. The streets are laid out in a grid so you can find your way around pretty easily. Hotter than hell in the summer."

"No snow?"

"Nope." Zena handed me fifty dollars. "Just to help you get started."

I felt guilty, like I shouldn't take the cash after I lied about how much I actually had. I shook my head and held up my hand to ward off the cash. "Why are you giving me money?"

"It's a way of keeping connected. I move around a lot. I don't write letters or remember birthdays."

I shook my head no.

"It's a loan, then, and I never forget a loan. I'll be passing through Phoenix real fast, but I'll stop in on my way back to collect the money you'll owe me."

"You're not staying in Phoenix?" I had assumed that everybody on a bus headed to Phoenix would be staying once they arrived.

"Hell, no. I'm on my way to New York. I'm just staying a few days with my aunt Ethel and then I'm on my way to the Big Apple." She pressed the money into my hand.

I tried to hide my disappointment. Leaving Alva seemed scarier when I was alone. I fingered the softness of the worn bills. "Any ideas of where I might get a place, something cheap, kind of safe?" I asked.

Zena frowned. "There're some neighborhoods in Phoenix you wouldn't want to be in after dark. It's a big city."

I licked my lips. "Your aunt have a big place?" I almost asked if she ever took in boarders. I was starting to feel a little naked without Alva. I hadn't slept alone in over five years.

"A little place, not much, but tidy."

I stared out the bus window watching the desert give way to shotgun bursts of building which grew thicker until you could be in practically any city in the country. I was two seconds away from asking if I could stay at Ethel's for a few days. I might have pleaded. I was getting that uneasy feeling you have when you see

where part of a highway has collapsed into a river. A sense of seeing but not believing, being afraid to take the next step, worried
that the earth might give way beneath your feet.

"Come with me to Aunt Ethel's. It'll be a way of balancing the
cosmic score. I cheated those two guys at cards, so now I'll do a
good deed." Zena smiled in satisfaction at seeing the scales of justice balance once again.

"I might have a little more cash than I first thought." Her offer
had propelled me into honesty.

Zena shrugged. "You'll be needing it."

Truth was, I didn't want to be Zena's good deed. I had been the
object of casual charity as a kid and it made me feel both not there
and too visible at the same time. But I did want company.

"Fifteen minutes until we arrive in Phoenix." The word spread
through the bus and heads bobbed as people started gathering their
stuff together. I checked my bag twice, making sure I had my
money.

The bus rolled into the depot in a haze of diesel fumes. I stood
up and stretched and waited as everyone shuffled off the bus slowly
as if all that sitting had frozen up their joints. Our bags were
stuffed in the very back of the luggage compartment. The porter
hauled them out, then closed the lid.

I followed Zena through the terminal, imitating the way she
gripped her bags. We passed through the glass doors and out to the
sidewalk where taxis were lined up together like a giant yellow
caterpillar. Zena grabbed the back door handle of the first cab.
"Let's live a little." She slid into the dull black vinyl seat. The driver, who had been leaning against the cab, took our bags and put
them in the trunk. I checked the name and picture on the hack license against the guy driving. They matched.

"We want to go to 17382 Laurel Falls."

The driver clacked down the meter and took off like the cops
were after him. I closed my eyes as he moved in and out of traffic.

Zena patted my knee. "Time is money in the cabbie business. I
used to drive one."

I opened my eyes to take a quick look at her. I had not yet been able to get a handle on when she told the truth and when she lied. Mostly I figured she lied.

We rode down streets crammed with businesses one right next to the other. I don't know what I expected—cowboys maybe, a cattle crossing. I saw cars covered with a fine dust and block walls streaked with graffiti. Some guy with tattoos on his beefy arm flipped off the cabbie, who answered back the same way. After a while, the buildings began to look newer and the houses all had the same kind of roof, like Monopoly houses all lined up.

"We're almost there," said Zena, sitting up straight. A few miles later, we entered an older area of brick homes with shingle roofs. Number 17382 Laurel Falls was a small bungalow with red petunias in large white pots lined up in front of a big window.

Zena punched the bell about eight times.

"Cut that out. She's going to be pissed before we even get inside."

"Nah, it's our secret signal."

Through a small window cut in the door, I glimpsed someone moving through the house in a brightly flowered caftan. When the front door swung open, I found myself looking into the face of the fattest woman I had ever seen. Her face seemed lost in the layers of fat around it. With the flowered caftan on, she looked like an animated cartoon flower, one with a human face.

"Zena, Bubeena, my baby." I lost sight of Zena there for a minute as the heavily fat-laden arms took her in. The movement of the caftan sent out the sweet scent of lilac.

When Zena emerged from the arms of Aunt Ethel, she turned to introduce me. "My friend Chloe. We met on the bus and you and I are going to help get her settled."

"Chloe, what a lovely name." Aunt Ethel swooped down on me and then I was lost in her embrace and the sea of fragrance that surrounded her. I must confess, I liked having her hold me like that. I felt safe, surrounded, cared for, like there was no other world beyond the world of Aunt Ethel's arms. When she released me, I fell back a step and mumbled, "Nice to meet you."

"Come in, come in." Aunt Ethel backed away from the door and we followed her into the house. The living room was huge, with an overstuffed blue sofa and two big recliners sitting on an Indian rug. A glass coffee table that had seashells embedded in the middle sat in front of the sofa. The wall across from the sofa had one of those giant-screen TVs, the kind where you can see the enlarged pores on the sports guy yakking at you about the game. To the left of the sofa, framed black-and-white photographs formed a triangle on the wall. The third wall had the largest print of Georgia O'Keeffe's *Sunflower* that I have ever seen. A vine rooted in a large ceramic pot grew up the fourth wall following a pattern of small nails.

"You kids hungry?" Aunt Ethel led us into the kitchen which was all white and gleamed with stainless steel pans hung up on racks over the stove. She pointed to the sturdy kitchen table with four wooden chairs, then motioned down with her hand. Zena and I sat. Aunt Ethel started a pot of coffee, then began pulling out sandwich bread and cold cuts. I wasn't that hungry yet, but I didn't want to seem rude. I wondered if Aunt Ethel would eat anything. Maybe the story that Zena told about the circus was true.

I looked around the kitchen. Besides the table at which we sat, there was only a large rattan chair with a moss green cushion over against the wall by the back door. The counters were empty except for the coffeepot and a toaster. The sink had a dish drainer holding a few bowls. The stove, with a ceramic flask full of utensils and a stack of oven mitts, looked new. The kitchen window was spotless and sunlight lit up the whole room.

"So, Zena, how goes it?" Ethel put a bowl of peaches on the table.

"I'm on my way to New York. Met this guy in Del Mar who was back for his father's funeral. Used to be a surfer boy and gave it all up to live in a brownstone and make money, but, catch this, he's a warlock."

"Be careful. New York ain't Phoenix."

"Yes, Aunt Ethel. And I'll brush my teeth, and make sure I change my underwear every day, and . . . and . . . and . . ."

"Don't be rude, or I'll sit on you, and you wouldn't want your boobies to be any smaller than they are."

Zena laughed. While Aunt Ethel's back was turned, I whispered, "Is she really your aunt?"

"Every ounce. She's been like a mother to me."

"What happened to your mother?" I'm always ready to hear mother stories, mine having crapped out when I was a little kid.

"Somebody had his dog riding in the flatbed of his pickup truck. He lost control of the truck on an overpass and the dog flew out and went through the windshield of my mother's car. She was driving right under the overpass."

I wanted to laugh. I could see this dog flying through space. "What kind of dog was it?"

"A Rottweiler. A smaller dog would probably have just cracked the windshield."

I waited for Zena to tell me it wasn't true. I watched Ethel fill a bowl with potato chips. I was looking for the twitch of a smile or a crescent moon of sadness on her face. Something to tell me whether or not Zena was lying. I wanted it to be a lie. Stuff like that was too strange. Life was shaky enough without dogs flying out of pickup trucks. Ethel's face was smooth, unreadable. Zena slapped two slices of turkey breast on the bread that Ethel had put on the table, spread mayo with a plastic knife, and took a big bite, then examined the tooth marks she had left.

"How old were you?"

"Five. Aunt Ethel took me in. Renamed me Zena. My birth name is Frances. Can you think of an uglier name?"

I could.

I didn't want to watch how much Aunt Ethel ate but I couldn't stop myself. I mentally counted every chip she ate and noted the refill on the soda. She didn't eat any more than I did. I felt ashamed for wondering.

"So, Zena, how long you staying? Until we settle your friend in? Maybe longer?" Aunt Ethel delicately patted at her lips with a cloth napkin.

"Not that long. I've got some business to take care of, then I'm out of here. You need any help down at the flower shop?"

Aunt Ethel gave me the once-over. She started at my hair which

needed combing and slid down to my sneakers which I have a
habit of scuffing up. "No," she said. I wasn't sure how I should feel
about her judgment. I liked flowers just fine. And once I got
cleaned up, I looked fine too.

"You two kids relax, take a walk around the block. You should
see the way the two guys who moved in on the corner have done
their house. I love it. Lots of color, they're from San Francisco. The
neighbors are going nuts. The house has been painted peach with
lime trim and has beds of pink petunias all over the yard. The city
used to be out here practically every week, writing up citations—
public health, zoning, cops giving tickets for illegally parked cars.
The old woman who used to live there would answer the door with
a baseball bat in her hand. These guys have a doorbell that sings
out 'Some Enchanted Evening.' The neighborhood could use a little color. Did I mention that they're black guys?"

Zena rolled her eyes. I couldn't tell if Ethel was telling the truth.
I wondered what Alva would think about two black, gay men who
painted their house in punchy pastels and had a singing doorbell.
Not much.

After lunch we were shown to a bedroom with twin beds both
covered in sunflower quilts. A bright yellow rug lay between the
beds. The walls were chalk white. A light pine dresser and a rock-
ing chair with a tufted forest green seat stood against the wall. The
closet was empty except for hangers, and Zena and I began to put
away our things. Zena unzipped her suitcase and called out, "I've
got the top two drawers." She quickly shifted her clothes into the
drawers, not bothering to refold clothes that hadn't been folded the
first time. I wondered if she knew how to iron. She pressed her
rumpled clothes into the drawers and forced them shut with her
leg. I carefully removed my clothes from my suitcase, putting the
underwear, socks, bras, and two pairs of jammies in one drawer in
neat, neighborly stacks. In the second drawer I put jeans, sweaters,
and my cosmetic bag. I slipped my personal stuff—an address
book, a small diary, and a red velvet jewelry pouch—underneath
my jeans. I slid the drawers shut slowly. Zena had hung up a purple
sequined cocktail dress and a black sheath cut practically to her

rear. My one good dress made of sensible cotton hung next to them like some shabby cousin in from the country.

After we finished, Zena showed me the rest of the house. Aunt Ethel had the bigger bedroom and a California king bed that took up most of the space. The bed had drawers built into the bottom, but most of the clothes seemed to be hung in the closet. Even the underwear was stacked in one of those shoe hangers. Probably easier to reach that way. Instead of a dining room, the house had a screened-in sunroom. Plants hung from hooks in the ceiling. Outside, orange trees littered the lawn with globe-shaped fruit.

I walked around the yard, jumping up trying to see over the six-foot block-wall fence.

Aunt Ethel called out from the sunporch, "I got to go to work now. I'll be back about five-thirty."

Zena said, "We'll make dinner. It'll be ready when you get home. Our treat."

"How sweet of you girls. Ta-ta. I'm off."

Zena turned toward me. "You can cook, can't you?"

I didn't answer.

"You do know how to buy groceries?" Zena questioned me with an upward motion of her palm.

"I can hardly wait." I didn't know why, but I was starting to feel bitchy, out of sorts.

"Are you homesick?"

"Not hardly." The truth was that I didn't want to cook dinner. Cooking dinner was dull and something that I had done for Alva every night for years. I hadn't left Alva to cook dinner for someone else. I watched a small green lizard do push-ups on the patio before scurrying into the bushes.

"I say you are. And I am at my most obnoxious when I am right, which lucky for you is pretty damn often."

"Fuck you." I rolled my lips up and outward when I said it. Gave the word the ugly feel it deserved.

"Not nice, not nice at all. It's OK to miss the one you ran away from."

"There's not that much to miss." I wanted her off my back.

"You miss what you got."

"What makes you think I ran away?" I narrowed my eyes in challenge.

"You got that busted-out look." She had that I-know-I'm-right smile.

I glared at Zena. I hated that she knew stuff about me as if I were one of those Visible Women with all my organs, blood pathways, and ropy muscles shining right through my plastic body. I should know more than I did. Why had I left Alva? Why was I missing him as if I had left behind my left leg? I knew I wasn't retarded or even slow. It was more like I just had these weights on me, like manacles or a ball and chain. Maybe it's because I didn't trust anybody, and although I thought I did, maybe I didn't trust myself either.

"Well, you're too old to be leaving your daddy, so I guess husband or boyfriend. What was it—drinking, gambling, chasing women?"

"None of that stuff, he just kept watching me like I was some kind of goddamn television."

For the first time since I had met Zena, I felt her interest in me sharpen like maybe I had more ingredients than she first thought.

"Husband or boyfriend?"

"Husband."

"They're harder to leave, the law gets in there. Any kids?"

"Just from his first marriage, they visit every other weekend."

"Why'd his first wife flake out?"

"She said he never paid enough attention to her. That and she had found Jesus."

Zena laughed, bending over and slapping her right thigh. "Don't you get it? She dumped him because he wouldn't pay attention to her and you dumped him because he wouldn't take his eyes off you. What a loser."

"Alva is not a loser. He's a perfectly kind man who deserves better than me." My voice rose up shrilly in his defense.

"Well then, I guess you did him a kind turn by leaving."

I retreated into silence, walking to the far corner of the yard where a stone statue of a rabbit peeked out at me from beneath a shrub.

In an incredulous but it's-so-obvious tone Zena said, "Don't tell me you never saw it that way."

I truly hadn't, but I didn't want to say so. I put away Zena's words to think about later. I didn't want to admit to anything that would make me look dumb.

The grocery store was brand new. No built-up dirt in the corner, no drooping plastic-bag holders. Zena stood in front of a mountain of lemons. "People are funny around here. They don't like different. They don't want to know your secrets. Just look like me and talk like me and I can be just fine with you—that's their motto."

I glanced at Zena. Her mouth had a bitter twist as if she had just sucked one of those lemons. "What's the matter?" I asked.

"After my mother died, none of the other kids would play with me. Their mamas wouldn't let them."

"Why?" I felt both outraged and puzzled at Zena's ostracism.

"I don't know. Maybe they thought death was catching."

I thought of the expression "catching your death of cold."

She added, "All I know is how alone I felt. Nobody would play with me and nobody forgot either, not for years until most of the neighbors had moved away. By then I didn't care anymore. I liked being alone too much." She tossed four lemons backhand into the shopping cart.

I knew that feeling: that being alone was the only safe place to be, and the only safe person to be with was yourself. I suppose that's why people finally do themselves in when they find that even being alone isn't safe anymore.

I knew the unvarnished truth when I heard it. Her words echoed off me, gaining strength with each bouncing sound. "I know what that feels like."

"I know you do."

Zena handed me a honeydew melon. I set it gently inside the cart and I followed patiently while she continued to cruise the produce section, picking up chili peppers, bagging garlic cloves, and rolling a ginger stick between her hands.

"Are you all right?" Zena's worried voice broke into the room in my head where I was arguing with myself about Alva. I stood squeezing a tomato. The juice and seeds had run down my arm and several people had stopped to stare.

"I'm fine, just fine." I put the squished tomato out of the sight under a bunch of grapes and followed Zena to the meat counter. We didn't talk again until we were out of the store.

Zena and I cooked up a fine meal for Aunt Ethel: a red-hot chili, cornbread, ginger-spiced melon balls, and chocolate cake for dessert. She did most of the cooking. I measured and searched through the drawers trying to find all the kitchen utensils that Zena felt she had to have to do the job right. After dinner, we cleaned up while Aunt Ethel went into the sunroom to do the books for her flower shop. I did a better job at dinner of not paying so much attention to what she ate.

Zena and I watched television in the living room on the giant screen enclosed in a wood cabinet that looked handmade. The overhead light began to flash on and off, and when we looked toward the doorway where the light switch was, there was Aunt Ethel, naked as could be. I couldn't take my eyes off her. I couldn't imagine the size of her body, the way the pounds had piled on top of each other till I could hardly believe she had bones. I thought she could roll herself down a hill and not feel much pain. She stood up straight, her breasts lying like two stretched-out water balloons on her stomach which swelled out like she could be gestating an elephant in there.

"You've been wondering and imagining what I look like, and that gets in your way of knowing me. So I'm going to show you. Then when you've seen enough of my body, you will be able to see me."

I'd like to say that I demurred, mumbled some kind of regrets and left the room, but I didn't. I stared. She turned around a few times like a model showing off a mink coat, stretching her arms out and swaying back and forth. Then she raised her arms, then bowed, making a real effort to touch her toes, but not getting any further than the top of her thighs. She gave me a modified beaver shot, the curly black hair creeping down her thighs, her legs Corinthian arches gone to bloat. Her body rippled with cellulite, putting me in mind of pocked, flesh-colored gelatin.

I said, "Thank you," and she turned and walked back to her bedroom, each buttock jiggling up and down with the movement.

I looked at Zena. She shrugged. "She's right, you know."

I knew, and I felt as if my better self had not been seen. I had been possessed by that dark part of ourselves that pulls us to follow the sound of screaming sirens, to stand behind the fire line and watch a building burn. The force that compels us to read every detail of some grisly story of abuse and then reread it. The need that glues us to our seats watching movies of women being terrorized and body parts meeting unconventional means of separation. I felt ashamed of myself. I wasn't at all sure that seeing Aunt Ethel naked would do anything to quell my morbid interest in her.

At ten, we shut off the television and took turns using the bathroom. I took the twin bed near the window. When I woke up, the digital clock glowed a green 6:00 A.M. at me. Zena was in bed with me, her hand touching mine in the lightest way.

Chapter Four

Abandonment is a difficult thing for most people to understand. My understanding of it is complete. It is in my bones and lives in my nerve endings and makes me feel that I never have to finish a book because I know how it will end.

Tom went to live with my mother's parents and so did baby Lucy. I never saw either of them again. I was mad at Tom for being the one they picked and at Lucy for being the baby they had to take, her being the baby and all.

My father was the kind of man to whom women are attracted who have learned not to look too closely at life. We traveled across the country in a brown Chevrolet Nova that had patches of rust; I called it Pinto after a horse in a storybook. The names and faces of the women changed like the scenery, but I can recall every single inch of the inside of that car.

The first time they left me at a rest stop, I was about six. I can't remember the name of the woman he was with but I do remember she had long blonde hair and I would sit in the middle of the back-seat rubbing my butt on the Indian blanket that covered the tears in the upholstery and think that maybe she was the Tooth Fairy. I sat there for hours watching the way the wind, coming through the window, blew her hair back. Sometimes I would focus on one strand of hair and just watch it and try to imagine where it would go next.

We parked. It was the first stop of the day and I had followed the woman as she walked with a sway in her step into the ladies' room. She never spoke much to me, though once she gave me a nub of lipstick that she couldn't roll down any further. I'd push my lips out and rub that nub round and round to get out a little bit of color.

The bathroom was concrete block and cold as a refrigerator. I used the toilet and washed my hands, wiping them on my shorts. I walked out stomping my feet on the concrete floor because I liked the echoing sound it made. I squinted in the sunlight and looked around for the woman. She didn't seem to be out yet, so I leaned against the wall and waited. I liked rest stops not just so I could stand up and walk but because people took their dogs and an occasional cat on a leash out of their cars, and I liked animals. I liked dogs best but cats were OK. After petting a dog, I would get in our car and close my eyes and press my hands into my hair and pretend that I was petting the dog again and that he was my dog and slept on my bed which, of course, had a canopy top and was in a house with a real roof and maybe an attic to hide in.

I wandered off to the fenced area where people let their animals off the leashes so they could run around. A man with white hair stood watching a small brown dog race around the perimeter of the fence yapping shrilly. I stood off to the side.

"You like dogs?" He smiled at me and held up the leash.

I nodded and turned my head to the side.

"Would you like to pet him?" He called the dog over and it had some sissy name like Muffy or something and he motioned for me to come closer.

The dog came up to the fence and I put my hand through to touch him. His fur felt soft and I could feel the wiggle of his behind right up to his head. He liked me, I could tell, and the feel of his tongue licking my hand sent shivers all the way up my arm.

"Where's your family?" The man's eyes looked past me like an army scout looking for smoke signals.

"In the bathroom, I think."

He let me walk the dog around on the leash. It felt good having that dog on the end of a leash, like the two of us were together, connected to each other, and I wanted to think that dog wouldn't take off even if the leash weren't there. That he would just want to stay with me, no matter what.

"Your family must be looking for you."

I ran back to the bathroom. I looked in all the stalls that weren't locked and peeked under the ones that were, looking for those pointed, high shoes that she liked to wear. I walked around the building twice and then started to cry. The man with the brown dog came over.

"What's the matter, honey?"

"I can't find them."

"Your family?"

I nodded, thinking that if Daddy came around the corner right now, I'd be in for a whipping for talking to a stranger.

"What color is your car? We'll just walk down to the parking lot and look for it."

We walked slowly toward the parking lot, side by side with the dog weaving between us, and looked through the lot row by row. Pinto was nowhere to be found.

"What's your daddy look like? I'll go look in the men's room. He might be in there."

I told him that Daddy was big and strong and had black hair and blue eyes. He said to come along and I waited outside while he went into the men's room but he came out alone with a funny look on his face. He said maybe we should look out back where the woods started, maybe they had gone back there for a little nap. It wasn't like my daddy to take a nap in the middle of the day. He wasn't much of a sleeper. Some nights he paced back and forth until the rhythm of his walking put me right to sleep. But I liked it that the man was smiling at me.

We headed out back and we walked so far that my legs got tired and he offered to carry me. He had slipped the collar off the dog and the animal zigzagged across the pine-needle-covered ground. I thought of asking him to put me down because I didn't like the way his hands were holding me, pressing into my bottom, but I did like being held.

Finally we stopped in a place so filled with trees, I could barely see the sky. "Let's rest." He put me down and slipped the collar and leash back on the dog who was by now stretched out on the ground panting with pleasure. The man tied the dog to a tree and took a candy bar out of his pocket. "You hungry?" I could feel my mouth water just looking at that candy. "Come sit by me." I sat next to him under a tree that two grown-ups couldn't put their arms around and watched him divide the candy bar. It pleased me greatly that he gave the bigger part to me. The day had warmed and the chocolate melted in my hands. I started to wipe my hands on the grass but he said, "Let me," and he began to lick the chocolate off my fingers. It tickled, especially when he licked between my fingers. He looked really happy. "Would you like some more candy?"

"Yes, please."

He gave me a whole candy bar this time and as I tore open the wrapper, he put his hand on my leg and as I savored each rich chocolatey bite, he moved his hand into my underpants. He moved his fingers around very gently and kept grinning at me. "You're a very pretty little girl. Would you like to be my little girl?" I nodded yes and put another bite of candy into my mouth and tried to think only about how sweet it tasted. "You know what I think the prettiest part of a little girl is? The part right where I have my hand, and I can tell by touching you that you're really beautiful, like a princess. Would you let me see it?" Without waiting for an answer he pulled down my underpants and just stared at my privates and I could see he was really happy. I held the last bite of the candy in my hand. I was starting to feel sick from all that chocolate when he said hoarsely, "Finish it," and while I was doing that, he put his mouth down there, and while it tickled me at first, after a while I felt really good. I don't remember how long I lay there, maybe I fell asleep. But the next thing I remember, I was alone in the woods and a five-dollar bill accordion-folded was next to my leg. It was then that I began to think about bears being in the woods and started to holler. Soon I could hear people shouting something back, but I kept yelling. When the young couple ran toward me from a wall of trees, I was just sitting there staring out into space with my face smeared with chocolate.

The man carried me back to the rest area while the woman jogged alongside and kept patting my hand and telling me that everything was going to be fine, that I wasn't lost anymore. A crowd had gathered. People asked me all kinds of questions: who was I, where was my mommy, what color was our car? It was then that I started to get scared. Being around too many people scared me. I wasn't used to being talked to so much.

A policeman appeared out of nowhere. "Now don't you worry, little girl, we're going to find your people and I'll let you put the lights on in my squad car and even use the siren."

Just then, the crowd split apart as Daddy pushed his way to the front.

"I thought she was in the backseat. I didn't even know she had gotten out. I only stopped to check my tires. Took right off, got a big job lined up in Tulsa and got to be there by Tuesday."

I don't think the policeman believed him. He asked for Daddy's identification and asked me twice if this was my father. He turned toward me and said sternly, "Don't you get out at rest stops without having somebody with you from now on, little girl." I nodded.

My father grabbed my hand and hauled me toward the car. I thought about how rough his hand felt. She was in the car, looking through a movie magazine.

She didn't say anything and neither did my father, but later that evening he gave me a swat for getting my dress dirty and my underpants all sticky.

Chapter Five

The morning was cool and the warmth of another body felt comforting in my sleep. I slept deep and hard, awakening slowly like coming up from a deep-sea dive. I became aware of body parts that were not my own. The feel of Zena's hip jutting up against mine, her hand resting upon my hand like a feather-light bird on a branch, our arms touching from shoulder to wrist. The sound of her breath coming in and out steadily without the slightest variation.

I didn't want to move. If I did, then she'd wake up or pretend to wake up and we'd both have to admit that she was in bed with me. I tried to sense the arrangement of my pajamas. Things seemed pretty much as they ought to be, though I couldn't really be sure without looking, and looking required moving.

I'd have to get up soon. The night had scoured my mouth to a sandy dryness. I had to have a drink.

Zena slipped out of bed in one fluid motion and walked to the bathroom without so much as a glance at me. I moved over into the center of the bed, reclaiming it for my own. I could hear the toilet flushing, the faucet running water, the creak of the door as she came out. I kept my eyes closed. She came out saying "good morning" in the most normal of tones. I decided to go with the flow, as they say. If she wasn't mentioning where she woke up, then neither was I.

"I'll make coffee."

"Great."

As Zena padded down the hall to the kitchen, I slipped out of bed and grabbed my jeans and shirt that I had draped over the end of the bed and picked out some fresh underwear and socks from the dresser. Zena had placed her sexy barely-there panties next to my sensible cotton ones. By the time I showed my face in the kitchen, Zena had brewed the coffee, started toast and eggs, and squeezed fresh orange juice. For my part, I had showered and dressed and felt armored for the day.

We both read the paper and ate in silence. Ethel had already left the house. Zena took a pen out of a kitchen drawer and began searching the classifieds.

I asked, "What's first, an apartment or a job?"

Zena looked up. "Let's see what kind of job you can get before you rent a place. You can use Ethel's phone number on your application."

I won't bore you with my job search. I met up with the usual you're overqualified, you're underqualified, you lack the right experience. I was looked up, down, and sideways. I wore a dress and panty hose and felt nothing at all like myself. For three days Zena drove me around in her aunt's specially adjusted car. The steering wheel came about six extra inches into the driver's seat, which had been pushed back as far as it would go. Pedal extenders capped both the brake and the accelerator. To drive the car, Zena had to roll the seat forward and drive hunched over because the steering column could not be shortened. It's like wearing high heels, she told me, her feet barely touching the pedal extenders.

We job-hunted in the morning and spent the afternoons helping Aunt Ethel at the shop. I liked the flower shop. She called it Fiona's Flowers. She said her middle name was Fiona—Ethel Fiona Finara. It was a small place wedged between a tuxedo rental store and a coffee shop. I always offered to run out for coffee. Two of my favorite smells are coffee and flowers. Fiona's Flowers was a long narrow room with a refrigerated unit behind the counter and a cash register. She made up the arrangements right in front of the customer. In slack time I'd walk around lifting up the planters and checking the prices. She had assorted forest animals, a few Blessed Marys with bowed heads, one Neptune holding a pitchfork with a square planter on his head, a naked couple kissing with a vase held between them, and several vases shaped like the heads of dogs.

I washed the front window, even did a funeral arrangement with Ethel's help for an old lady whose first name had been Luz. I made deliveries with Zena when Ethel's high school boy couldn't come in because of midterms. I learned a lot about plants and flowers, and even though every night I went to sleep alone, every morning Zena was in bed with me and neither of us had anything to say about it.

One night Ethel took us out to dinner. After dinner Ethel ordered brandy that came in snifters big enough to put goldfish in.

"Ethel, you ever really truly in the circus?" Brandy seemed to speed up my natural curiosity as much as it stumbled my tongue.

"Never. That's one of Zena's stories. I'm a glandular case, though nobody believes much in them."

"Was Zena's mother ever in the circus?"

"No, the poor darling. My sister had disastrous taste in men. She kind of fell apart after her third marriage."

"You took Zena in?"

"Yes, I did. I tried to be a mama to her but I don't know how well I did."

Zena said nothing.

"Is Zena a lover of women?" I heard the question but wasn't sure that I had asked it.

"I believe she is, but perhaps you should ask her yourself."

I wanted to turn to face Zena but the effort seemed overwhelming. The brandy flowed like molten iron in my body, filling me with heat. Forming words had become like shifting concrete blocks around in some complicated, ever-changing pattern. "Are you a lover of women, Zena?" It seemed like forever to get that sentence out and even longer before Zena replied. When she did answer, I had to think for a moment about what the question had been.

"Yes, I am."

Once I connected the answer to the question, like two boxcars in a railroad yard, I felt calm because, to my way of thinking, nothing beats knowing what's going on.

Zena came into my bed again that night. She didn't wait until I had fallen asleep. The brandy had made things feel slippery to me, like everything was just a little bit beyond my reach. Her lips were soft at first, then harder, and I tried to focus on the inside of my eyelids, trying to make colors appear like silent fireworks. I felt her breath on my cheek and her lips nibbling at my right ear. I started to giggle. She let go of my ear and kissed my left breast. I let my breath out without taking any in. I got dizzy. I did what I do best, I just kind of left my body and stood hovering over myself and Zena. When she removed my nightgown and kissed her way from my forehead to my feet, I began to shiver. She pulled the covers over me while she stripped out of her pajamas. Our bodies felt good together, like we were both featherweights, not like one of us was trying to get the other to take up less space. A woman's hand on me was sweet. Her hand brushed back my hair as if I were a sick child having a fever checked. I wanted her to never stop touching me. I was like some parched field opening up to receive a thunderous rain. I didn't care what she touched, only that she not stop. Every place she touched me, I lit up, glowing with my own incandescent energy. Being cared for, caressed with gentle hands, my soul massaged, squeezed in the most pleasant of ways.

She began to move against me with a motion that jarred my pillowed thoughts. Her weight became heavy and I wanted to throw her off but I didn't. I resumed my vigil overhead and watched her rub against me.

My cheek was wet. There were tears on her face. "Don't cry," she said. I touched my face. The tears were mine. I held her tightly and buried my head in her neck and only when she pried my hands away did I relax my grip.

We lay together silently for a while and my head has never been emptier. I felt like I was starting over in some new, yet-to-be discovered way.

When Zena got up to shut off the light, she climbed back into her own bed on the other side of the room. I wanted her to stay with me. I wanted not to be alone.

In the morning when I awoke, Zena was up and gone. Packed her bag and off to New York. She left an envelope with Ethel who handed it to me after I poured my coffee. I pulled out the single sheet of paper and unfolded it. Written on Fiona's Flowers stationery in simple block letters was "I love you, Zena."

Ethel had looked away when I opened the envelope. As I slipped the note into my back pocket, she turned to me and said, "I love her deeply, but she'll bring you nothing but grief."

"It's not like that, Ethel."

She only nodded and waddled out of the kitchen.

I stayed with Ethel for two weeks. I worked in the flower shop in the mornings and spent my afternoons contemplating my future. Things weren't easier to sort out away from Alva. Even though he wasn't actually in the room, I could feel his vibes across the hundreds of miles that separated us. I called three times. A woman answered the phone each time, even when I called at one in the morning. Alva's mother had died, and I knew it wasn't his ex-wife's voice—she had a hillbilly twang. I could hear the squeak the bed made when Alva rolled over to the side I usually slept on, the side closer to the phone. I didn't say anything, just hung on the line while the woman said hello-hello into the line, her voice growing shriller with each hello. Then she hung up. I guessed that Alva was done missing me. I didn't like the idea that Alva had my replacement already. I didn't want him, but I sure liked the idea that he wanted me. I decided to get one of those Do-It-Yourself Divorce kits, fill it out, and mail it to Alva.

You'd think that finding Alva so recovered from my leaving would make me feel better, relieve my conscience a bit, but it didn't. I wanted to go back and find the two of them in bed together and blow their brains out. What Alva had done was hurting me more than my leaving had hurt him, I was sure of that. I had my freedom, but I had it at the cost of being dumped. Even if I had been the first one to leave, I still felt dumped. And I was entirely too familiar with the feeling. All my life I'd been left behind while others went about their lives. I'd been alone so much that being alone felt natural and being with others felt like being pressed into the center of a crowd full of tall people and not being able to see anything, not even when I jumped up. The world was told to me through the words of others and the sight of others. Daddy told me who I was (nobody) and what could be expected of me (nothing) and the kind of person I was (not at all good). I was messed up beyond description and lost to redemption, or so they said.

Working mornings at the flower shop, I put out the white metal flower cart that we filled with the bargains of the day, cleaned the front window, and watered plants. I also dusted planters and checked leaves for signs of unwanted guests. In the afternoon I went back to Ethel's house, lay on my bed, and trotted out my sorrow tightly bridled, cantering over my heart leaving a crisscross of paper-cut thin lines. Then I'd cry and fall asleep and not wake up until Ethel pulled in the driveway at six. She never asked me what I did in the afternoon and she handled most of the dinner conversation, just directing me as needed in making the dinner and cleaning up. I followed instructions well. One night she said to me, "How long is this going to last?"

"What?"

"This grieving."

"Alva has another woman. I've called three times and she always picks up, even late at night." My voice shook with self-pity.

"Some men just can't sleep alone." Ethel could have been delivering the weather forecast, clear skies, balmy day.

"I thought that he couldn't live without me."

"So why'd you leave, then?" Ethel sat across from me, stacks of thin silver bracelets coiling about her arms.

"It wouldn't last. Good stuff never lasts."

"You saw to it that came true, didn't you?"

"I figured better to be the leaver than the leftee, but if he has a new woman . . ."

"Was Alva good for you?"

I said no—but felt twice as bitter knowing that, although things hadn't been good for me, I had been replaced faster than a pair of windshield wipers. I used my fork to corral the peas on my plate into a circle.

"So what are you going to do?"

I shrugged and flattened the peas into a green blob.

Ethel pushed the apple pie toward me. I took the last piece, not asking if she wanted seconds.

My life still felt too heavy. Shedding Alva hadn't been enough. Having a woman make love to me tapped deep into me, but I wasn't sure that I was meant to be a lover of women. I knew myself well enough to know that Zena could be a man, woman, or android. The gentle touching was what I craved. The feeling that I was cherished. I hadn't much experience with being cherished but something inside me knew what it was. Some kind of survival thing kept drawing me toward the flame, though my experience told me that things never end well.

I still felt all plugged up, full of stuff I wanted to cough up. I read Zena's note at least a hundred times, but nothing's cheaper than saying "I love you"—a greeting card sentiment.

I figured Ethel would start watching me like Alva had. She'd start expecting things from me. I wasn't staying. I wasn't five years old anymore, I could leave too. The highway of life now ran east and west. I wasn't stuck waiting for a father I was afraid of to come home. My big brother wasn't threatening me with the bogeyman if I cried. I wasn't going to cry. I was moving on.

Alva had forgotten me and I'd forget Alva.

I slipped on my backpack and tucked my hair under a baseball cap. I'd compressed my belongings into the backpack, telling Ethel I'd be back someday to pick up the rest of my stuff. I figured she'd get tired of holding my things and Goodwill them.

Ethel dropped me off by the highway. "Take care now, honey,

come back soon and remember that what's inside you ain't the whole world, though it might feel that way."

I waved her off and stood watching the old Buick as it sagged its way back home.

The way the dark clouds scudded on the horizon, I didn't much care who picked me up as long as I wasn't standing on the road when the rain came.

My first ride was in a semi. It takes a long time for one of those babies to stop and I ran toward him as he pulled over, his brakes making a high-pitched sound. "Where you heading?" He was a big man who leaned over and pushed the door open.

"Anywhere warm."

"Hop right in. I'm heading to Mexico by way of San Diego."

I said "thanks" and hauled myself into the cab filled with the crackle of his CB.

"My name's Jake."

"I'm Bobbie." I didn't want to use my real name. I put my back-pack between my feet. We pulled out and I looked down at the rest of the world from the high and roomy cab. Kind of like being on a ski lift.

"I'm hauling milk."

I hadn't given any thought to what he might be hauling. I only knew it wasn't cattle or pigs because the sides weren't slatted and it didn't smell bad. I was glad not to be riding in front of twenty thousand gallons of gas or a ton of nuclear waste.

After a few minutes of silence, Jake started talking about base-ball teams, then politics. I didn't really need to answer, just to move my head up and down. I unbuttoned my jacket. During a lull in the talk, I asked him, "How long will it take you to get to Mexico?"

"Not as long as you think; I have my little friends to help me." He held up a bottle filled with blue and white pills.

"What are they?"

"Speed, other names. Depends on your dealer. I know this one guy who makes up his own names for them—his private stock, he says. I don't use him much. I saw him talking to his dick in the john one night."

It was then that I realized that Jake thought I was a guy. I had never been mistaken for a guy before, at least not that anybody told me about. But maybe that was why I couldn't stay with Alva, and why Zena made love to me. Maybe I wasn't "all woman."

"You want one?" Jake held the bottle out toward me with thick fingers tipped with blackened nails. Even his finger pads had dark striated swirls. "I like my company to be awake."

I took one and washed it down with some coffee from a silver thermos he pointed to on the seat.

"We'll stop in a couple hours for lunch. My treat."

What the hell—a ride to Mexico, the opportunity to take illicit drugs, and a free lunch. Things were going well.

As I sat up in that cab and looked down at the people in the cars, I had a funny feeling. Like I was peeping into windows or through keyholes. People think they have a kind of privacy in their cars that they don't really have. Think of how many times you have seen people pick their noses while driving. People act like they aren't surrounded by glass on all four sides or that you're just too damn busy driving your car to notice what they're doing. I saw things from my perch that surprised me. You wouldn't believe how many people perform unsafe sex acts at sixty-five miles per hour, and I'm not talking here about not using a rubber. Jake pointed them out to me and gave a blast on his horn as we barreled past. I was definitely seeing the world. When something especially interesting came into sight, Jake would slow down and slip back in behind them so that we could get a better view. They liked that, they really did. Some of them waved real friendly-like. One woman, with her skirt up to her neck and nothing on underneath, kept licking her lips and then sticking her tongue out at me. Maybe this looking-like-a-boy thing had gone too far.

"She likes you, son." Jake chuckled and for the first time I noticed his teeth, which were small and perfectly shaped and as white as bicarbonate. The woman in the car gestured to the right as if she were hitchhiking.

"What does she want?" There she was in front of us, licking her lips and sticking her tongue out and pointing wildly to the right.

"She wants us to pull over in the rest stop and get better ac-
quainted. The driver is kind of hard to figure with that cowboy hat
on, could be a man or a woman. For some of these folks, it's not an
important difference."

"Are we stopping?" I could hear the quaver in my own voice,
just when I thought things were going well.

"Hell, no. I got to get this load to Mexico and pick up another
and head back. She probably has lice, traveling livestock." Jake
reached over and patted my knee.

I moved closer to the truck door and felt for the handle, just in
case. It was there; it hadn't been sawed off. I was glad I had taken
the pill. Falling asleep didn't seem like such a good idea anymore.

The pill made me feel alert. I noticed everything, I couldn't stop
looking, my ears picked up every sound, I felt twitchy but definitely awake.

A line of chatter came over the CB, from people with names
like Buffalo Bob and Bill Beaver using lots of words that sounded
like codes. "What are they saying?" I asked.

"Lots of talk. I only listen for the important stuff like bad
weather, cops, accidents, weigh stations where folks are looking
the other way."

I listened to the CB for a while. The choppy sound of voices
jarred me but I supposed it offered comfort out here on the rib-
boned road, especially at night when there was less to see.

"Sometimes I listen to country-and-western. You like that music?"

In truth I hated C&W, but I wanted to stay on Jake's good side
and said yes. In return for my deceit I got to listen to a full hour of
lamenting over cheating husbands who just couldn't help themselves and cheating wives who wanted to be let off at the corner so
the old man wouldn't find out. An hour of soul-wrenching misery
where even the happy songs sounded sad to me.

About one o'clock we pulled into a truck stop and Jake parked
next to a cattle truck "because though it don't smell good, hardly
anybody ever parks on the other side, so it's easy to get out."

Jake knew a few people there and apparently didn't notice the

fact that I used the ladies' room when he went to the gents' because
he still called me "son" when he told me to order anything I
wanted. I ordered the Big John Tough Trucker plate, which came
with a giant burger, a slew of fries, extra pickles, and your choice
of drink. I took a Dr. Pepper thinking about the upper, which made
me start laughing until Jake kicked me right in the knee and I
stopped. "Don't go getting goofy on me, son. The cops eat here
too." I looked around but didn't see any. Could Alva have sicced
the cops on me? Said I stole money from him or something?
Thinking about Alva took all the humor out of drinking Dr. Pepper
while buzzed on pep pills.

Jake talked to a few men but didn't introduce me. Several of the
drivers looked at me and then quickly looked away. It gave me a
funny feeling. I ate everything on my plate including the extra
pickles and felt uncomfortably full.

After lunch I went to the ladies' room again while Jake went to
warm his rig. When I came out, Jake was standing there with a surprised look on his face. He didn't touch my knee after that and he
didn't talk about sports. Mostly he was quiet when we hit the road
again except for about fifteen minutes when he started talking
about his ex-wife.

"I never knew what she wanted." His voice when he talked
about his wife wasn't as loose as when he was pointing out naked
people to me.

"It can be hard," I agreed.

"Came home early from a run one night and found her in bed
with one of my drinking buddies."

"What did you do?"

"I hit him over the head with a bottle and chased my wife bare-
ass naked out of the house. I took it hard."

"And then?"

"I packed my bag and left before he came to or she came back."

"Any kids?"

"No, and I'm grateful for that. Otherwise, I'd have the damn
government on my tail hounding me for money for them."

"That's a tough break." No sooner had the words left my mouth than I realized that I sounded just like Alva. That was the kind of thing he used to say to me when I tried to explain these feelings I had about not being able to breathe or swim any further when I wasn't even in the water.

"I hear from her sometimes. She sends letters to the company I work for. Wants me to come back and try again. I can't. A man's got his pride."

After this, Jake fell into a prickly silence and stared down at the road as it began to get dark.

"You hungry?"

"No, I feel OK, real alert."

"Thanks to my friends, we won't have to stop except to piss before we hit San Diego."

I shifted my butt in the seat and regretted the coming darkness.

Jake started to talk again as night spread across the country. I don't know if it was the darkness or the uppers—I'd seen him take another one—but he just didn't shut up. I wanted him to shut up. I had my own little conversations going on in my head and I couldn't seem to keep a thought straight for all his talking.

I had never thought of myself to be like Alva. I had come to see Alva as the opposite of myself. That was the only way he could control me the way he did, because he wasn't at all like me. I always felt myself the odd one, the one with too much feeling or too much thinking or too much supposing going on inside me. I was always excessive, overreacting, seeing things that to Alva just plain weren't there. It bothered me something terrible when he'd tell me that things weren't the way I saw them, especially since so much of me was tied up with what I saw. I had to believe in me. All my life, I'd been the only reliable person in my life. If I couldn't rely on me, what could I do?

We pulled into San Diego about six-thirty. I'd been awake for close to thirty-six hours. The night before I left Ethel's place, I'd been so keyed up with leaving and not knowing where I was going, I hadn't been able to sleep. My skin felt crawly like it was just an envelope for some alive thing inside me that wanted to get out.

"You're on your own now. I'm not taking you across the border. Thanks for the company and the advice."

I didn't remember giving any advice but I said, "You're welcome."

"I'm going to get a little sleep after I hit Mexico, got another little friend. Want one?"

"If I don't take one, how long will I be like this?"

"Too long, trust me."

I took the pill Jake gave me and drank it down with the last of the now cold black coffee. I decided not to take any more pills for a while. I felt really bad.

"You'll be asleep soon. There's a YWCA in town and here's ten bucks. I went through your backpack and I know you ain't a guy."

I must have looked shocked that he had gone through my backpack.

"Well, you can't expect me to take you practically to Mexico without knowing a little something about you. Even when you're high, you don't talk much."

I said nothing, having learned a long time ago that the best place to keep oneself is to oneself. I stepped back from the truck as the tires churned up gravel pulling back onto the road. I waved goodbye and he blasted his horn. I could smell the ocean. I walked in off the road feeling the sucking sound cars and trucks made passing me.

I took a city bus to the Y. I hoped that everything was still in my backpack.

Chapter Six

Daddy told everybody that my mama was dead. Grown-ups liked me better when they heard my mama was dead. I could see them softening right in front of me, the shoulders slumping forward, and with lowered voices they'd offer me a nickel or a bit of candy or a stick of gum. Sometimes I'd tell people that she was dead because I liked the way the air changed about me when the words came out of my mouth, like a spell, "My mama died." It made me feel special.

A truant officer came around one evening when Daddy had been working steady and asked why I wasn't in school. It was late spring and the turquoise blue lights of the motel sign blinked into the night.

"Didn't know you fellows worked nights." Daddy tipped his kitchenette chair against the wall.

"We don't. I'm kind of doing this on my own time."

I sat on the sidewalk keeping an eye out for lightning bugs. I had washed out a mayonnaise jar and punched holes in the lid with a rusty nail I had found out back. I could feel the truant officer watching me.

"How come she's not in school?" He stood over Daddy and looked down on him.

"She's stupid. You can't teach her nothing."

"What happened to her?"

"Killed her mother coming out. Must be God's work."

I didn't look up.

"She looks bright enough to me." The officer squatted down in front of me. "What's your name, sweetheart?"

I could smell coffee on his breath and I wanted to tell him everything he wanted to know, but out of the corner of my eye I could see Daddy making a slashing motion across his throat, so I said nothing.

"How old are you, sugar?"

I liked his eyes and I liked the way he had stood over Daddy, looking down at him. "I'm eight." I offered up my answer while staring at my dusty toes as I burrowed them into the soft earth.

"She belongs in school even if she isn't too bright." He stood up and I could hear his joints creaking. "Your school is Mountain View, have her enrolled by next week or I'll be back." He turned to me, "Just about time for those bugs to be out. A girl that can catch bugs can go to school. You'll like it there."

He started across the parking lot and hollered out, "I'll be back."

He may have come back. The next day we moved to the other side of town, and in a few months it was summer. I turned nine that June and although Daddy didn't remember that it was my birthday, I did find a dollar on the sidewalk which I took as a positive sign of being nine.

I wasn't stupid. Starting that fall, I called the truant officer all the time on myself, using dimes that I stole from Daddy. He got tired of them coming around and sent me to school because he "didn't like messing with nobody with officer in his job title."

I won my first contest that fall. I won a school book bag from the drugstore on First Street. They had it in the front window propped up next to a Mason jar full of pennies. You had to guess how many pennies were in the jar. The bag came with notebook paper, a mechanical pencil, erasers, and the one thing I loved the best, a box of colored pencils. I guessed four hundred pennies. The fountain boy gave me a scrap of paper. I wrote down my guess, put my name right underneath, then folded the piece of paper in half. I stuffed it into the empty ice cream tub just like he told me to. Monday, when I walked down to the drugstore to get cigarettes for Daddy, I saw a red arrow with my name in fancy writing pointing to the book bag and I knew it was mine.

Chapter Seven

The lobby at the YWCA had a chandelier that sparkled light and a fountain that sounded like stones plinking into shallow water. The woman at the front desk told me a bed cost eight bucks a night plus a little extra for sheets and towels. They had to be changed once a week. Male guests were to be entertained in the parlor. I felt like I was in some fancy old-time hotel. I liked being in a place for women only. It made me feel safe.

My room was small but clean. Square-shaped with a bed, dresser, and an overstuffed armchair. The lights all had working bulbs and the place appeared quiet. I picked up my towels and went in to take a shower. The community bathroom fluoresced such a bright white, it felt like being in the inside of a giant's mouth full of cold, hard feeling. The water ran hot and the soap dispenser leaked tiny beads of gray liquid. After showering and combing out my hair, I started to feel the pill that Jake had given me. I suddenly was really tired, as if I had been awake for a lifetime instead of a day and a half. In my room, I hung up my wet towel and pulled the shade all the way to the bottom of the window. I crawled beneath my covers hardly disturbing the tightly made bed. Sleep came with the closing of my eyelids.

I awoke to the sound of women's voices seeping into my head

which felt like dry rot. I couldn't bring myself to get up and face a bunch of women probably all with someplace to go who'd stare at me and ask questions.

Things quieted down as I lay in bed and played my little game of assigning life stories to people, except this time I could only hear their voices. It's much harder to do that way. When the sound died down, I got out of bed and walked along the hallway in my nightgown to the john. It was empty except for one stall on the end where I heard someone coughing.

As I stood at the sink studying my face, which looked surprisingly young to me, as if leaving Alva had been a form of cosmetic surgery, I saw a woman bent over from the waist crab-walking across the floor.

"Are you OK?"

"Fine, it's just my period. It's been like this since I started."

"You need any help? Back to your room?"

She slowly straightened and I could see the red-rimmed eyes and puffed-up nose. It was hard to tell exactly what kind of face it was, streaked with tears and twisted up in pain.

"Do you have any aspirin?"

I did, and after walking her to her room the way you've seen old people walked down the corridors of hospitals, I ran back and took the aspirin out of the right pocket of my backpack.

Her room looked just like mine with her window closed and shade drawn. It took a minute for my eyes to adjust to the dark. I picked up a glass from the dresser and filled it with water from the fountain just outside her room. "Convenient having that water fountain next to your room." I couldn't think of anything else to say.

"Not really. People hang around and talk when I'm trying to sleep."

I figured her for about twenty-five. She had wavy blonde hair down to her shoulders. She sat on the edge of her bed. She took the aspirin and threw her head back to make it go down with the least amount of water. "I have to get to work. I'll lose my job if I don't."

"What's your job?"

"I make checkbook covers. Usually I operate the machine that melts the vinyl together, then I rip off the outer edge." Her hands mimicked the motions. I felt like we were playing charades.

"Good luck. I hope you feel better."

"I got an idea. How about you take my place today and I'll let you have the money? They pay by the day and I'll get to keep my job."

I had all kinds of questions but she kept talking. "My name is Patsy, so call yourself that. They don't really care who shows up, just that the work gets done. Foreman yells out 'Patsy' and you step up. I've only been there a few days, they won't remember what I look like."

"I don't know." I started to back out of the room.

She talked faster, like a train was bearing down on her and her foot was caught in the track. And she grabbed my arm. "If I lose this job, I won't be able to get my kid back from welfare. I've got to prove that I've changed."

"But you can't help having a bad period." I wanted her to let go of my arm. I could feel her nails digging into me.

"They don't care what the reason is. Once you get with them, everything is your fault anyway. You should have planned ahead, you should have an-ti-ci-pated this development. None of them ever done a bad thing, I don't think they even shit in the morning."

"Let go of my arm. I'll do it. I need the money."

"The Lord bless you. You got bus money?"

"I do."

"My shift starts at ten. They keep funny hours. Take Bus 25, get off at Lone Peach Tree Road, the place is right across the street, there's a sign. I'm going back to bed." She turned, feeling for the foot of the bed like a blind person and then passing her hands over the spread in search of the pillow. Once in, she pulled the covers up right over her head. I said "good-bye" to a white mound and went back to my room.

I dressed in my last clean jeans, shirt, and underwear and headed out. I didn't see how I could lose anything if they paid in cash.

The building sat back from the road and formed long clean lines of white brick with sooty-looking windows like blackened eyes. The place wasn't noisy but it had a terrible smell about it, kind of like living inside a cheap vinyl wallet. They did make checkbook covers, but the job started at seven-thirty, not at ten. I explained things the best I could and, because the First National Bank of some backwater town in Florida had sent in a massive order, I was allowed to stay. Hell, I was ordered to stay. I think they would have blocked my way if I had tried to leave.

A woman named Sylvia showed me around the place and I paid close attention to anywhere that looked out of the way and shadowy where a Woody could hide. I am the sort who learns from experience. Sylvia had a chin and a nose that narrowed to the same point with a beauty mark on her upper lip that looked like a pencil mark. She had about her an angular appearance as if someone had created her by following a learn-to-draw book but hadn't gone beyond the first few pages. Her eyes were the same deep brown color as the beauty mark and she had long thick lashes. If you could see only her eyes, you might find her attractive.

She sat me down at a stool attached to a press over six feet high. Standing next to me, she laid down a small sheet of vinyl, pulled her hand back, and pressed the button at my right side. A hot plate came down and melted a square in the vinyl. She picked up the hot vinyl and tore off the outer edge and stacked it on top of a pile of vinyl squares. "Work fast, don't talk, keep your eyes on your machine." Sylvia pulled a picture out of her apron, a color photo of what looked like raw meat. "This is what happens if you don't pay attention."

I looked at the picture. I'd be paying attention. If it weren't for the nails at the end of that slab, I wouldn't have known it was a hand.

"This is the emergency button." Sylvia pointed to a red button to my right. I would have to lean forward to reach it. The low-level room noise, a mind-eating kind, swelled in volume at I stared at the photograph. "Get started." Sylvia squeezed my shoulder before walking away.

I watched her pink-sweatered back go down the aisle of killer machines and I felt scared. I looked at the other women on the line but none of them looked at me. They kept their eyes straight ahead on the press while their hands pulled out hot squares and tore the outer edges off.

I'd start out slow. I was new. I could work my way up. I tried to close everyone out and develop my own pace for the job. I kept looking at the emergency button. I even tried it once to make sure it worked. I could see in my mind's eye what my hand would look like pressed into a bloody red square. I had to stop thinking about that in order to keep working. I poured all my concentration into getting the job done.

When the noon whistle blew, the whole place shut down with the hiss of a giant snake. People sounds began to take the place of machine mutters and I looked around, thinking that I hadn't brought any lunch. A gray-haired lady nodded toward the front door. "The lunch wagon comes in about five minutes. Don't get the egg salad. You wash up over here." I followed her to a ladies' room that had a long brown vinyl sofa pushed up against one wall. The place smelled of cigarettes, and the john doors slammed as they closed.

I tagged behind a line of ladies to head back outside to stand in another line to wait my turn at Bertha's Lunch Bucket. I played it safe and took a peanut butter and jelly sandwich, milk, and a chocolate chip cookie. The gray-haired lady came over and sat across from me at one of a row of wide-planked picnic benches that had been thoughtfully supplied for the employees. She poured a handful of sunflower seeds on my plastic wrap and asked me my name.

"You're new, aren't you?"

"I'm just helping out a friend."

"What's her name?"

"Patsy. She's staying at the Y too."

"What's her problem?"

"Bad period. Thanks for the sunflower seeds."

When I mentioned The Curse, it was as if I had touched on some ancient current that ran through all women. She smiled and touched herself sympathetically somewhere below her belly button. I'd seen old guys pull at themselves and blame tight underwear, but I had never seen an old lady acknowledge that she had any body parts below the neck. I felt embarrassed for her. Once she found out I wasn't staying, she started asking questions about Patsy, most of which I didn't have the answers to, so I made stuff up. Maybe when Patsy did return, this woman would be prepared to impart to her whatever age-old wisdom was hers to pass on: "don't think about it, the pain will go away" or "have another baby." She certainly wouldn't suggest "have an orgasm" or "do yoga."

I ate my sandwich and looked around. I wondered how much they paid. I wondered if Patsy would feel better by tomorrow. I didn't want to come back. Even the outside had that awful smell as if the trees grew plastic leaves. I touched one to make sure it was real. The leaf had a fine white dust from the parking lot graveled with white stone. The leaf was both lifelike and real. Some real things do not at all have the feel of life.

I spent the afternoon being as careful as I had in the morning, though the afternoon sun poured in the windows and heated the place up and made me feel drowsy. At four-thirty the quitting bell sounded and I followed the example of the others as they cleaned up their work stations. Then we walked single file toward the exit, stopping right outside the entrance while the owner, Mr. Samuels, had a few kindly words with each employee and handed out an envelope. I think the words were kindly, for most of them smiled when they took their money. He gave an especially big grin to a blonde and a pat on her back that drifted slowly down toward her rear. The others seemed not to notice. When my turn came, he looked at me with slit-sized blue eyes and said, "I do hope Patsy will be coming back soon."

"I'm sure she will," I optimistically offered and put my hand out for the envelope. When he handed it to me, his eyes opened all the way into blue orbs and the whites around them were veined with red lines. His hand felt slick like he used baby oil.

Within five minutes the parking lot was empty and I stood waiting for the bus. I was hoping that I wouldn't meet up with anyone else and could just get on the bus and head back. Contrary to the way my life usually goes, the bus pulled up as if taken right out of my imagination. Swaying as I walked down the aisle, I found a seat toward the back. I laid my head against the warm bus window and closed my eyes to the speckled dirt on the glass. After a few minutes I lifted my shirt sleeve and gave it a sniff. I smelled like vinyl. I hoped it would wash out. I opened the envelope and took out forty dollars, not bad for a day's work, and my hands looked OK except for a little reddening of the fingers at the very tips of my right hand.

I stopped by Patsy's room and found her sitting in bed having a smoke and looking a lot better. I asked, "You'll be going back to work tomorrow, right?"

"Right. Old Patsy is feeling much better." Old Patsy couldn't have been much older than twenty. Her face had smoothed out and she smiled at me.

"Do you need any of this money?" I felt kind of stupid offering her part of my pay, but it seemed the right thing to do.

"No, I'm fine. In fact, I'm doing real well. Went down to Western Union and my cousin wired me money, so I'm set for the week. Thanks for doing the job for me. Work that pays cash is the best."

"Cash is king."

As I turned to go down to my room, she asked me, "Do you smoke?"

I said no, I had never gotten the habit.

"Not that kind of smoke, the other kind."

"Not much."

"Come back about ten o'clock to my room. I got a job interview at nine tonight. We'll girl-talk."

"OK."

I walked down the hall toward my room and hoped that by ten o'clock I'd be sound asleep. And sure enough, by ten o'clock, I was asleep. But that didn't stop Patsy from rat-tat-tatting at my door. I stumbled out of bed and opened up.

"It's about time," she hissed.

"What is it?" I leaned against the door jamb.

"Come down to my room. I've got some great stuff."

"What?"

"Pinwheels."

I said, "That stuff sticks to my teeth."

Patsy whispered, "I have a six-pack of beer."

I told her, "I'm really tired."

Patsy grabbed my hand and pulled me down the hall to her room. I was starting to feel sick from being awakened suddenly. When we reached her room, I flopped on the bed intending to go right to sleep. Patsy started to talk. Sometimes I mumbled stuff like "yeah" and "sure." When I'd feel myself starting to drift off, sleep a sweet siren song, Patsy would poke me or tickle the bottom of my feet.

Patsy's bed was softer than mine. She sat cross-legged on the floor, her back up against the wall. She had a small metal ashtray in her hand, and the smoke haloed her head. She asked me twice, "What's your story?"

"No story."

"Yes there is. Who you running from? What man? Your boyfriend, husband, father, brother, cousin?"

"What makes you think it's a man?"

"You know any women who run from other women?" She pulled in a deep breath of smoke.

"Women are not saints. My own mother left me when I was five."

"She wasn't running from someone, some guy, your dad maybe?" She exhaled, but only a wisp of smoke came out.

"No excuse." My words came out slower, stretched out like taffy.

Patsy repeated, "Who you running from?"

"My husband."

"He beats you."

"No."

"He cheats."

"No."

"He gambles . . . drinks . . . likes other men . . . does dope . . . what the hell does he do?"

"He watches me."

Patsy nodded her head like she understood, but I knew she didn't.

I woke up in Patsy's room but she was already gone. She'd left a hand-rolled joint in an envelope covered in scribbling that looked like a grocery list. I tried to decipher some message for me but found none. I sealed the envelope and left it on her pillow and went back to my room. I had spent the entire night dreaming about Alva. Alva as a giant baby wearing a diaper and crying for me. Alva hunting me down, siccing private detectives on me. Wanted posters stuck on telephone poles—MISSING ONE WIFE / SEEMED HAPPY ENOUGH / I DIDN'T DO ANYTHING WRONG / WHAT DO WOMEN WANT ANYWAY NOWADAYS?—with me stark-faced in black and white staring out, with my description and date of birth neatly lettered below. Now the whole world would know that a thirty-year-old woman, 5 feet 4 inches weighing 140 pounds, had left Alva Edward Herson. Last seen at the breakfast table serenely smiling over a cup of coffee. Foul play suspected.

Maybe Alva wasn't that bad. I mean, he really wasn't. But all my life, I've needed to feel free. I'd spent too much time in a box. When I married Alva, I thought I'd like staying in the same place, knowing what would happen next. Feeling safe, I liked that, but somewhere along the line feeling safe changed to feeling dead. Like nobody could hurt me, not because I was finally safe but because I wasn't alive anymore.

By noon, I stood next to a merging traffic sign with my thumb stuck out. Lots of traffic, semis groaning by, their wheels sending up flurries of road trash and grit stinging my eyes. When I saw one coming, I stuck my thumb out and narrowed my eyes. I was hoping for a ride with a woman trucker. I had seen a few on the road but most seemed to come with husbands or boyfriends.

The first person to stop was a fat guy with a box of donuts on the seat next to him. He was a good bet in that I could surely out-run him, and the donuts looked good. But he was only heading a

few miles out and I didn't want to be looking for another ride so
soon. I watched his head bob up and down, a chocolate-covered
donut jammed in his mouth, as he pulled back into traffic. I was
hoping for someone going a long way, someone harmless. Do
those people pick up hitchhikers or is it only the odd and deranged
who require the company of strangers on long stretches of highway?

The sun was starting to warm me up when a blue sedan with a
fresh wash job rolled onto the pavement about thirty feet in front of
me. I walked quickly and when I came abreast of the car I noticed
that the interior had little lace doilies covering the backseat. The
woman at the wheel wore what I hoped was a badly combed wig
and red lipstick. Her age I figured to be somewhere between fifty
and seventy. The fact that no lipstick was smeared on her teeth I
took to be a good sign.

"Where you heading?" She ended her sentence with a lilt.

"Your direction."

"I'm going as far as Los Angeles to see my daughter, she just
had a baby."

I took that to be an invitation and climbed into the car, keeping
my backpack between my legs. She waited until I put on my seat
belt and cautiously moved back into the traffic.

"Mind if we stop a few times? I've got low blood sugar and I
have to keep my food coming in steady."

"No problem."

"If you get too hot or cold, let me know."

"Thank you."

She introduced herself as MaryBelle, saying she had spent her
life in the South and had nothing to show for it except "this damn
accent and the best-ever recipe for mint juleps."

I told her my name was Alana and that I was from Alaska.
Alaska was full of people but I'd never met anyone from there. I
don't think anyone ever left Alaska and it was the kind of place
I could make up wild stories about and no one would catch on. I
liked that kind of freedom. I thought of it as the "elasticity of real-
ity." Alva always told me that I was real smart and that if I had "ap-
plied" myself, I might have become someone.

When I didn't talk, MaryBelle and I fell into a companionable silence and I read the road signs and mile markers, while looking at the dead animals flung on the side of the road. I took a long look at MaryBelle. She was even uglier than I had at first suspected, and I'm not at all the kind of woman who passes that kind of judgment on other women. I've always felt that the standard of beauty for women is harsher than for men and she was a case in point. As a woman, she was a loser, but she might have made an OK-looking man as long as she didn't put on one of those big bellies. You know the kind, who look like they're about to drop a full-grown Holstein on the front lawn. If I were a man and had one of those watermelons gone wild, I wouldn't be drawing attention to it by wearing a tight T-shirt and pants with a waist two inches too small. I guess some of those guys don't own mirrors.

"Let's stop for a snack." MaryBelle was already turning into the lane to get off and seemed to know exactly where she was heading. "I'll be just a minute. You want to get out and look around?" She had pulled into the truck-stop area and seemed pleased at the number of trucks in the lot. I decided to walk over to the john and left MaryBelle examining her makeup in a gold-plated compact with the initials M.B.C. in curlicue letters. When I returned ten minutes later, after having whacked a vending machine into giving me a package of cookies that I had paid for, MaryBelle was not in her car. I ate my cookies standing next to it. When I looked around, I saw her getting out of a neon green semi. Her wig was a little off center, and even from this distance I could see that lipstick was smeared on her face. Her slip hung down from her dress showing me about three inches of lace. She dropped down from the truck and landed on her bare stocking feet, her heels in her right hand. I turned away to climb back into the car. I wondered how much she charged.

As she walked to the car, she pulled her dress back down over her hips and firmly pressed her wig back into place. Once in the car, she turned the rearview mirror with a practiced twist and took a tissue to her smeared lips. She made a final adjustment to her wig and smiled at me. "A friend from high school, a very good friend, haven't seen him in years, just ran right into him."

"Life is full of the unexpected." Another Alva-ism.

We rode on, the car reeking of sex. I had to open the window and let air blow into the car. MaryBelle turned up the air conditioning.

"I do what I have to do," MaryBelle offered up as if the very silence in the car were filled with questions.

"I understand."

"I've been this way since I was a little kid."

That part I didn't understand but this was a free ride.

"I always wanted to be just like my mama. She always looked so good and smelled like flowers even when she was dying. I never wanted to be like my daddy. He was mean and dirty and just plain vulgar. He thought amusement meant farting at the dinner table and persuasion meant hitting."

I closed my eyes.

MaryBelle's voice deepened. "Daddy never loved me. He never even liked me. Said I was a big sissy for sticking up for Mama. Once I begged her to paint my nails—she had this wonderful color called Passion Pink—and, of course, she did. When Daddy found out, well, he like to hit the ceiling. He threw away all her polish and said that if she ever did anything like that to his son again, he'd throw her right out too. Then he said he had to make a man out of me and took me behind the house and shot my dog and said if I started to cry, he would shoot me next." MaryBelle began to sniffle.

I said, "Don't cry, you'll make your mascara run. You'll look like a raccoon." Her being a him didn't come as a complete shock to me.

MaryBelle sucked back the sadness.

I asked, "What happened to the old bastard?"

"He stepped on a rusty nail and died of tetanus."

Stories like that always make me think that maybe there is some justice in the world even if it isn't well distributed.

"You don't think I'm some kind of perv, do you?" MaryBelle's voice trembled.

"I can't say I understand you, but you're no stranger than some I've known."

"Do you still want to ride with me?"

"Sure, but do I still call you MaryBelle?"

"No, call me Billy. That's my real name and it could go either way."

When he said "either way," I had to laugh.

I rode with Billy all the way to Los Angeles and he even let me drive for a while. He liked to talk about makeup and offered to do me up if I had the time. I told him that I thought he ought to save up for a better wig. He agreed. "The synthetics are crap. Best ones are made with real human hair, virgins from Thailand, I've heard."

He talked about loving his mother so much, wanting only to be a woman and hating his thing so bad that he'd tie it back with a piece of clothesline and a diaper, pretending that he didn't have one. Growing up I hadn't felt much like either a male or a female. Sometimes when I thought of myself, I'd picture a brain, a pile of gray matter where words and ideas traveled convoluted paths. I liked when Billy talked about his mother. There comes a point sometimes in listening to people where you are ready to believe anything they tell you. You have passed into them and become them and sometimes it takes a long, long time to go back to being you and even then part of them is always in you like a sliver.

Billy dropped me off on the road near a restaurant. Easier to catch a ride, he said, and shook my hand just right. He didn't squeeze like he was wringing it out or barely touch me like I was a reptile.

"You have nice hands," I told him.

He smiled and said, "Thank you, I use the extra-strength hand cream—unscented, of course, so it won't clash with my cologne." He unclasped his purse, a baggy tan vinyl, reached in, and handed me a sample bottle of Gentle Care Extra-Strength Hand Lotion.

I waved as he flipped on his left turn signal and pulled back onto the road. I appreciated the advice, being as I had never grown up with a mother and mostly everything I learned about being a woman came from reading books and watching television. I put the small bottle in my jeans pocket.

Los Angeles had a different feel than Phoenix. Things here

seemed to be going warp speed, highways twisting like snakes having seizures. The cars zoomed faster than the colored displays on video games. The restaurant appeared to be the place to go while I figured out my next move.

It was close to 5:00 P.M. and I decided to check out the cheapo motel attached to the restaurant. The striped canopy at the entrance snapped loud as thunder as a cold wind began to cut through my clothes. Listening to Billy had been hard for me. People talking about their mothers called up a sadness in me that waited like a dog for a door to be opened.

"I need a room just for the night."

The desk clerk acted like he was headed for a movie career and this job was just something to be laughed about once he became a star. He looked at me for a minute as if he thought I were plying my trade—as if I were the true female version of Billy. He must have decided that I lacked the qualifications for any degree of success in that field. Turning the registration book toward me, he intoned, "Ten dollars for the night. You want to be close to the office or *not?*"

"Close to the office, *please.*"

Once I said that, his opinion of me seemed to improve and he held open the door for me against a wind that blew hard enough to bring snow down from the North Pole.

Number 3 was just three doors down from the office and had a better smell than I expected. Things looked clean enough but I didn't bother to turn on all the lights. I flicked on the television. I asked the boy if a laundry room was available. "Just past number ten but don't go there after dark, this ain't Kansas." He laughed out loud at his humor but he laughed alone.

I decided that I needed to eat.

It was the kind of restaurant where they show you what you hope is plastic food under a glass top. You have to admire the lifelike browning of the lettuce leaves, though, and the soft white puddle of whipped cream on the custard. It took a while for the hostess to notice me, as if I didn't take up enough space by myself and surely I must be waiting to be joined by others—a herd of women all returning from the bathroom. Or perhaps she thought I was

waiting for a man, who by virtue of his sex would make me visible
to her.

Finally her eyes roved my way and I locked gazes with her with
what I hoped was a modicum of mind control on my part. She
picked up two menus as if she still couldn't believe I was alone. I
followed her, skirting empty tables, to a minibooth meant for two.
She put down two menus. She almost had me believing I wouldn't
be eating alone. I sat down, putting my paper napkin on my lap. A
little sign at my table said if I wanted water, I had to ask for it. The
man across from me picked up his fork, licked it, then dried it off
with his napkin. He then repeated the process with his spoon and
knife. He looked normal. In a lineup of people suspected of tongu-
ing their silverware, he wouldn't be my first or even third choice. I
kept glancing over to see what he might do next, but he acted OK
except for licking his silverware, which was kind of disappointing.
I ordered the Swiss steak with green beans and fries. I ate too fast
and didn't leave a tip. My waitress kissed up to every guy in the
place while I had to ask four times for the ketchup.

After dinner I walked over to the lobby to get some quarters and
picked up my complimentary postcard that in no way resembled
the place I was staying. Maybe it was one of those past-life postcards. This was, after all, California. Back at my room I gathered
up my laundry and stuffed a pen in my pocket. The wind had died
down, and after I started the washer, I wrote a note to Alva on the
postcard.

Dear Alva,
It wasn't personal. Remember to take your vitamins. Only
feed the fish once a day. Hope you and your new love are
happy. I was mad at first but I think I'm over that.
Yours,

Chloe

The clock radio glowed 8:00 A.M. at me but the room was dark. I
could hear the slash of rain and a distant growl of thunder. I
climbed out of bed and the floor beneath my feet felt cool. I pulled

open the curtains. All the color had been sucked out of the world, the sky clouded as gray as the atomic dust in a black-and-white movie. I heaved a sigh. Rain always made me feel sad. The muffled sound of voices and car doors closing came through a shroud of dampness. Rain subdued the world for me. I didn't like it much, too many things were left unseen. Rain brought up a feeling of deadness in me. All things muted. When I couldn't hear myself, I depended on the sounds of the world to keep me a part of it. Rain made me feel like a small bird struggling to live.

I walked down to the motel office to get my free cup of coffee and kept close to the building. The lobby smelled of aftershave. The man at the desk looked about forty with a receding hairline that would be a memory in a few years. I poured my Styrofoam cup full of coffee and sat down to read a newspaper that someone had left. As I sat there, the desk clerk took one call after another, his half of the first call ending with, "Well, see you tomorrow." By the third call, he was screaming into the phone, "So what if it's raining? You stupid enough to believe it never rains here? You can't believe the lyrics to songs. You people all shoulda stayed in your own country. Who's gonna clean those rooms? You don't think I'm gonna, do you? Show up or you're fired."

I asked, "You need somebody to clean rooms?"

He looked over at me and said, "Fifty bucks and tips, you have to do twenty rooms."

I figured he was probably taking advantage of me, but on a day like today I wanted to be busy. "And my room free for tonight."

He looked at me like I was cheating him but said, "Sure, I'll write it off as a vacancy."

I cleaned twenty rooms but only made ten bucks in tips and some of those rooms were absolutely disgusting. Knotted condoms floating in the toilet, sometimes two or three. In all the rooms I cleaned, I don't think any single person went without sex the night before. If I didn't find condoms, I found the bedsheets twisted up or the TV on the cable channel that shows smutty movies. I worked wearing plastic gloves. I looked under the beds and in the closets but I never found anything worth keeping or likely to bring a reward for its return. I played detective and tried to deduce from the clues where the people who had been there were going after they checked out. A phone book left open provided a clue especially if it was open to the business pages. The work was hard, and if I had been an extraterrestrial checking out Earth people, they wouldn't get very high marks for orderly living.

I ate in the same restaurant that evening, having skipped lunch to get the rooms ready by check-in time. I studied my dining companions for odd behavior but they all seemed to be busy talking to each other. Halfway through my bowl of vegetable soup, I started thinking about Alva and how he'd pick the peas out of his soup using a spoon. He said he liked the flavor of peas but not the peas themselves. I knew that cleaning filthy motel rooms was not an improvement on cleaning up after Alva. At least with Alva, I didn't eat alone in restaurants. I was having sex even if the sex was only so-so. I used to keep lists of things I did and read them over at night, proving to myself I had spent my day well and not just drifted through it like a mindless captive of time. The meal gave me heartburn and I realized I had no place to go and nothing special to do.

I picked up my pay from the movie-star night clerk, who passed me the cash with a twisty little smile like he knew what I'd done to get that money. I told him in a concerned voice, "I think you got a crater of a zit coming up there on your chin."

I watched TV in my room until I fell asleep. I told myself I wanted to be on the road by eight in the morning. I knew I'd wake up on time. The thought would rattle in my head all night, entering my dreams like a chant, "up by eight, don't be late."

I turned down three rides before I took one with a little old lady with gray sneakers and white sports socks and a coat that hung off her body like an XL dress on an undersized mannequin.

"God bless you."

"You too." I hadn't sneezed. "Thank you."

For an old lady she drove fast and I found myself watching the road and pushing my foot down on a nonexistent brake pedal. I said, "You're going kind of fast."

"God is with me. I have no fear."

"It still might be a good idea to slow down." I checked in the side-view mirror for cops.

Like a two-year-old stuck on opposites, she flattened her foot to the floor and I watched the speedometer skyrocket to eighty-five. I think I felt the chassis of the car start to shake. Now I really wanted to see a cop with a quota to fill or a warrant for the old lady when she suddenly took her foot off the gas and let the car coast to thirty-five miles per hour.

"I'm getting off here. I got some Lord's work to do."

Before I could say "Let me off on the highway," she punched the gas pedal and zoomed down the off ramp, rolling right past a stop sign into the dirt parking lot of the Spirit of Sunshine Church. It looked a lot like most other small churches, white with a simple cross atop, almost as if they were all assembled out of the same kit or as if some bigger white church had given birth. Several old cars in the lot looked as if they hadn't run in years and belonged up on blocks, but to my surprise their doors opened and so many people tumbled out, I thought it was a trick and somehow they were reentering the car on the other side and changing clothes just to fool me. Sometimes my thoughts worried me.

One of the men called out to her. "Miss Ida, you're looking fine. The Lord be with you."

Miss Ida got out of her car flexing her back with one hand on her tailbone. "You can help," she told me. I frowned, getting a story ready. She added, "It's the right thing."

I followed her inside to a room paneled floor-to-ceiling in an oily oak finish that looked as if just touching it would slick up your fingers. There was an altar made from a hollow-core door resting on two sawhorses, partly covered with a white cloth. Flowers on the altar filled the room with a sweetish smell of decay. The building had no windows. The only light came from one overhead lamp.

As if she could read my mind, Miss Ida offered by way of explanation, "Saves on the heating and cooling bills."

I followed the litany of instructions as Miss Ida took charge of the twenty or so people in the church. We hauled in folding chairs and wiped all the seats down. I sorted brochures and set them out on a long narrow table up near the entrance. The titles were catchy: "Don't Hit the Road, Just Lighten Your Load with Jesus" and "Don't Put It in the Bank, Be Saved with Jesus" and "Twenty Questions for Sinners." Two bone-skinny men with their wrists dangling from their shirtsleeves kept looking at me like they knew I was planning my escape.

"Get right with Jesus, sister," one of the men called out to me, raising his head like a divining rod pointing straight at my sinfulness.

I was definitely in the wrong place. God had always been a disappointment to me as had most of His two-legged creatures. I had been doing the right thing for my whole damn life and had nothing to show for it. Daddy had cheated, lied, and been meaner than a slow-acting poison, yet he spent the last ten years of his life baking on a beach in south Florida and accepting casseroles from well-meaning but desperate old women. Did he take their offerings, squeeze their oversized butts or "accidentally" touch their sagging breasts, and then on a Saturday night pay for a young woman? I only knew he was dead when somebody, I don't know who, maybe one of the casserole ladies, sent me his obituary from the *South Floridian Times*. There was no mention of me in the obituary and there wouldn't have been one except that he had married some woman with the biggest collection of pennies in the state.

So all this believing felt too much to me like Daddy talking to me, me taking in his words like dye into the cloth of my being. I made myself proud by fooling Daddy, calling the truant officer on myself. I studied hard, learned everything even if I thought I'd never need to use the information. Filled my head up with facts and spewed them out on test papers and volleyed the answers to the questions of my teachers. But now I wasn't in school anymore. All the knowledge that had settled into my head was making it unbearably heavy—some days a burden I longed to be rid of.

People started to sit down. One of the bone-skinny men sat in a folding chair pressing his lips to a harmonica, and notes flowed into the room. More people had entered, their body heat warming the room. Voices lowered. Candles glowed light into each corner.

I didn't believe much in God. He had certainly never answered my prayers, though I had prayed plenty. I had offered Him up sacrifices. Like all my hair when I was nine, I just cut it all off with a pair of dull scissors. Another time I had stuck myself one hundred times with a straight pin all over my body and not cried once while the little dots of blood measled my body. Nothing worked. Sacrifices hadn't moved Him, doing good hadn't moved Him. When it came to hearing my voice, God had his Walkman on extra loud. That was my state of belief. And being in church, even a made-up church like this one, spooked me. Not believing in God is a really scary thing.

I began stepping backwards toward the exit, keeping my eyes on the altar, where one of the women in a blue dress had started shaking for the Lord. I grabbed my backpack at the front door and heard Miss Ida yell, "Where you going?" I just started running and didn't stop until I reached the highway even though I knew that no one followed me.

I wasn't going to trade Alva for God.

I knew I had come as far as I could. To the south was Mexico and I couldn't speak Spanish, to the north was cold rain and snow, to the west lay the ocean. The pressure of choice was upon me. I was going back to Ethel's. It was the warmest place I had ever been.

I put my thumb out and hoped for the perfect ride.

Chapter Eight

I had always hoped, on a sky full of stars and an occasional four-leaf clover, that my mother would come back to me. That somehow, somewhere, like a divine revelation, she would realize how much I needed her. I had to accept that she had left of her own will. She hadn't been sucked out of my life by a god having a slow day. She should have taken me. I wouldn't have been much trouble. Her leaving left such a big hole inside of me. A hole around which the rest of me grew while the hole stayed the same size. It never got any smaller and if it were any larger I would have imploded from grief.

I looked at women on the street, searching their faces for something of myself, thinking that maybe if one of them looked enough like me, she might be my mother or—upon seeing the resemblance between us, like Narcissus and the pond—she would fall in love with me and want me with her forever.

My desire made me stupid.

There was one woman who I thought looked a lot like me. She had dark brown, almost black hair, and eyes just the same shade of blue as mine. I followed her around for a while in town one day while she went from store to store filling up her shopping bag, a straw bag with plastic flowers. Sometimes I waited outside the store, sometimes I went in and looked around, always keeping her in sight. She didn't notice me. In the fabric store, I watched her matching buttons to the ones she held in her left hand while I pretended to look at a revolving rack of thread.

At the grocery store, she picked up ten apples, turning each one over like the Earth passing a day, before she decided on the ones she liked. She paid out of a brocaded change purse and counted the coins out in precise movements. Having the correct change and not having to break a bill appeared to please her. Her bag grew heavier and I wanted to offer to carry it for her. She then went into the law offices of Himmer and Sloton, sat down in the waiting area with her bag on the seat next to her. A few minutes later, a man in a business suit came out smiling and led her to a corner office. I walked back and forth waiting for her to come out. When she came out, she was smiling and swinging the bag full of her purchases like they weren't heavy anymore. She noticed me right away and smiled. I took a chance. I ran up to her.

"Why are you following me?" Her voice seemed amused.

I looked down. I thought I had been clever. "No reason."

"Well, please stop. You must have something better to do with your time."

I hadn't, but adults hated to hear that little bit of truth. I nodded in agreement. She turned away. I blurted out, "I thought you might be my mother."

"I never had any children. I couldn't possibly be your mother."

"Would you like one?" I used my most polite voice.

"One what?" Her voice had gone up a bit in impatience.

"One child." I answered like I was giving the correct answer to a math problem.

"Goodness, no, and I'm certain your mother wouldn't want to let you go."

I decided to play my ace in the hole.

"My mother died when I was little, from the flu."

Her smile dropped off her face like a mask and I could see the narrowness of her eyes. "Well, that's a sad story, little girl, but I really have to be going." Nothing else, no smile, no nickel, no softening. As she walked down the sidewalk, she kept turning around to make sure that I wasn't following her. I stood watching her, thinking that she would change her mind before I lost sight of her. She didn't. She turned the corner by the drugstore and was gone.

This was the first time the dead-mother story hadn't worked. Was nine too old to still need a mother? Was I not wretched enough anymore? I had always counted on that story to get me sympathy. The thought that it no longer worked filled me with a hard-edged worry. The pity of strangers was about the only softness in my life, and being without it made me feel like I was being crushed to death between two stones, like some martyred saint. I wasn't brave enough not to cry out.

I decided that the woman was indeed my mother or at least a relative who couldn't bring herself to acknowledge that I was real—a nightmare given flesh and placed before her. I walked around town every free minute I had away from school. For the next month, I searched for her. I looked in stores and banks, passing cars and beauty salons. I stood outside the law office, shading my eyes to look in through the lettered window. One day, in desperation, I pulled the door open and walked in. The same man who had shown her to the back office walked by with a coffee cup that read "Interest pays."

"Mister, I'm looking for a lady with a straw bag, you showed her to that office over there. I need to talk to her."

He stopped, his brow scrunched up like he was trying to remember something. "You must be that child who was bothering her on the street." I didn't want to admit to anything so I kept quiet. "What's your name, young lady?" I said nothing. After a minute of him giving me his best threatening look, he raised his right arm and pointed toward the front door. "Please leave." I walked out backwards, keeping my eyes on him as if memorizing his every feature. He sucked in his gut and lowered his head like he had horns and was about to go after me. I pushed into the door with my shoulder blade and fell out into the afternoon sunshine and took off running down the street.

Daddy lost his job the day after that for drinking and we left
town in the night, leaving our motel bill unpaid. I never saw that
woman again, but when I think of my mother, that woman comes
to mind.

Chapter Nine

Ethel didn't ask any questions when I returned, just smiled and told me that I had enough road grime on me to change my country of origin. I kind of wanted her to ask me where I'd gone, what had happened, but then I liked just being let back in, like maybe in some way this was where I belonged.

Ethel wasn't much on small talk. She saved that for her flowers and plants, assuring me that talking to them helped them grow. I learned lots about Ethel from listening to her chatter away at her stock. She said that certain plants had certain listening characteristics, like roses were basically sympathetic since they knew about the thorns in life. Yellow roses were the kiss-off flower. Someone sends you yellow roses and it's over, baby. Yellow carnations were the flower of disdain.

In general, yellow didn't seem a positive color for flowers. That bothered me a lot. It seemed a contrary concept, like flying fish. I loved the color yellow, the brighter the better. I'd turn into the color yellow if offered the choice. Bright yellow pulsed with energy for me—kind of a reverse kryptonite.

Ethel kept a book under the counter that told you all about the meaning of flowers. Daisies meant innocence. Petunias, which Ethel had planted around her house, meant "never despair." She

said lilies had the hand of God on them so their meaning was
sweetness and purity.

If the coffee shop next door ever went belly-up or the tux place
on the other side, she wanted to take that space and expand with
more flowering houseplants.

"What will you call the new place?" I'd finished watering the
ivy and ferns and stood in front of the refrigerated case studying
the way the cut roses unfurled their petals.

"A completely new name. It will be a new start for me. I believe
in new starts. We can start again if we go about it the right way."

"What way is that?"

"Well, my mother, God bless her, always said, 'You don't move
into a new house without making sure the old one is swept clean.'"

I didn't say anything, just started dusting the planters, but I was
thinking.

The phone rang late in the afternoon. Ethel sat in the easy chair,
out of sight of the customers, and reached over to pick up the
portable that she kept nearby. "I'm glad to hear that, baby. Either
Chloe or I will pick you up. Flight 722, arriving at 8 P.M., got it. I
know, this coming Tuesday."

Ethel pushed herself up from the chair, knuckling the armrests.
"Zena's coming back. You want to pick her up or should I? We
have a while, she's not coming until next Tuesday." I fingered a silk
flower and said nothing. Ethel said, "We'll decide later. How about
going out to lunch, my treat? We'll throw a little business to the
place next door. Maybe he'd like to order carnations at discount for
the dinner trade." I nodded. Zena returning had typhooned my insides.

The Second Cup Coffee Shop looked like early morning no
matter what time of day or night you went in there. Breakfast was
served all day long so the smell of pancakes and bacon never left
the place. The TV in the corner brought in only one channel, the
twenty-four-hour news channel, or so the waitresses told you. The
dinner menu offered the usual meat loaf and spaghetti but ordering
breakfast made you feel like you were doing the right thing.

The place was so lit up that darkness came as a surprise when

you opened the door at night. The waitresses, suffering from per-
petual perkiness, always acted like today was really the first day of
their lives. Like every day was a new start, just scrape that grill
clean and start frying. But the food was decent, and the coffee was
strong enough to give the spineless a backbone and sent me out the
door in overdrive.

I looked around. "Business is good, Ethel. I don't think he's
moving out soon." I noticed the grease spots on the menu.

"Well, I happen to know that the owner hasn't stuck with anything longer than two years, and that time is coming right up."

"People change." I decided to order the ranchero special. If you
had a lousy day, you could come in here late in the afternoon, order
breakfast, and pretend the day was just starting.

"Not as much as they *don't* change."

The waitress brought a carafe of coffee. I creamed my coffee to
a milky tan. Ethel and I sat in silence. Zena's return sat on the table
between us, like some oversized box that you couldn't see over
without standing up. "So, you want to pick her up?" Ethel looked
down at her empty sugar packets, which she was busy pleating into
neat lines and then folding in half and stuffing into her empty
cream container.

"No." I slid my empty sugar packets toward her side of the table.

"She may not even come back, the girl's unreliable."

I mined Ethel's voice for meaning. I replayed her words in my
head again and again. I wanted her to say that she liked things just
as they were, the two of us. Ethel smiled at me and said, "You can
leave the tip." I took that as a good sign.

Now that Zena might be coming back in less than a week, I started
asking Ethel questions. I had the feeling that Zena returning might
mean Ethel leaving in some way. I wanted to pull Ethel closer to
my own orbit. It has always been my thought that I learn more
from listening to others than from telling my own sad little story.
Plus I don't like anyone to see me cry. I never cried in front of
Daddy or his girlfriends or my teachers or anybody.

I learned early on that the safest place for me was inside me, my own fortress of flesh, my laser beam mind searching the world for danger. Maybe I saw more danger than was actually there—kind of a seat belt of the mind, but it was all I knew to do for myself.

"What was your mother like, Ethel?" Ethel sat at one end of the sofa, me at the other. We were watching the news.

"Skinny."

"And?"

"She didn't like me being fat. My nickname was Peanut when I was in the second grade and weighed in at my first hundred pounds. She'd go through my room after I left for school looking for hidden food. Lifting up my mattress, going through my drawers, opening all the shoe boxes. She'd put everything back, but I always knew that she'd been there."

I asked, "Did she ever find food?"

"Once or twice. I was very careful."

"Where did you hide it?" I passed the caramel corn to Ethel. She put both hands in and ate right out of her cupped hands.

"In a small box the same color as the shingles on the house, kind of dirt brown. I had the box all tied up with fishing line and hanging off a nail right outside my window. My room faced the back of the house with a big old tree right next to it. She never saw it, not ever." Ethel smiled at her victory.

"What did you keep in the box?"

"Tootsie Rolls, Bulls-Eyes, Spearmint Leaves—that kind of stuff. In the winter, I'd put the frozen candy in my mouth and just let it melt in there and ooze right into me until I felt quiet inside again."

"When my Daddy got drunk, I'd steal change from his pants pockets to buy candy."

"My mother never drank, said it wasn't ladylike."

"Ethel, did you think your mother was pretty?"

She sighed. "Prettier than me."

I wondered if most girls thought themselves prettier than their mothers. My only pictures of my mother were in my mind. They were fuzzy and taken of a stranger.

"How about your mother, Chloe? You're a good-looking woman, bet your mama was too."

"Don't remember. Let's change the channel." I pointed toward the TV with my chin.

Ethel announced, "I'm going to get some more caramel corn."

"I'll get it for you." I was up and on my way to the kitchen before Ethel could get off the sofa.

She accused me, "You know, you're depriving me of the only exercise I ever get."

"That is not true and you know it." I shook the caramel corn out of the bag, a jumbo five-pound size, until it was empty. Then I compressed the plastic into a small ball which I tossed into the can. Talking about my mother made me want to eat buckets of caramel corn.

Ethel clicked the remote control to the educational channel, which was showing a special on psychic phenomena. "I don't believe any of that stuff," Ethel offered between chews of caramel corn.

I said, "I believe most everything I hear, at least at first. Kind of like I need to believe in everything because I probably don't believe in anything."

"To my way of thinking, believing is both the easiest thing to do and the hardest at the same time," Ethel said.

"Ethel, what do you believe in?" I'd never asked anyone that before. It seemed too personal.

"I believe that you're just coming to life."

I snorted. Ethel talked crazy sometimes.

I liked living with Ethel. Although Ethel weighed more than two Alvas, I didn't feel her presence the way I had Alva's. Alva acted like the routines of daily life were as set as a fossil in limestone. Alva's voice kept coming to me now at the oddest times, like when I'd spill the sugar or make a wrong turn heading for a delivery. His voice sounded different. I'd hear him call me "dumbo" or "retard" or "klutzy," and I'd think how that wasn't a very nice thing to say to me. I hadn't thought much about it at the time. In truth I'd agreed with him. I could be a real bonehead. But now I saw things differently. It wasn't fair for him to say those things to me. I never laughed at him when he'd stand bent over in front of the refrigerator saying he couldn't find the potatoes, even though there they were, lying big as life, on the bottom shelf.

"I think you daydreamed your way straight through that psychic show." Ethel stood at the sink letting the small fan that she had screwed to the wall blow air on her face. Ethel could work up quite a sweat without much effort, but then just moving her body took work.

"I know."

"You miss Alva?" she asked.

"Only on cool mornings," I joked.

"No, really, do you?"

"Sometimes I do, but I don't really know why."

Ethel let the dishwater out of the sink and stared down at the retreating foamy water. "Sometimes people miss pain. It's a strange, dark thing, but I've seen it."

"You're too deep for me, Ethel." I did that a lot. I made jokes when someone came too close to the alive part of me.

"You miss your daddy?" Ethel rinsed the dishrag and wiped the sink clean.

"No way."

"How about your mama?"

"Can't miss what you never had. I miss her the way I miss my mansion and my pet pony, Pinky."

"You're lying about your mama." Ethel snapped off the fan and walked into the living room.

I was pissed. "I am not lying. You're trying to make something out of nothing. You've been watching too many of those shrinky talk shows." Ethel had settled herself on the sofa—I could hear the hiss of air as the cushions sank in. I wasn't going to watch television with that woman. That bitch. She had called me a liar. I ought to just pack my bag and split. I stomped down the hall to my room, locked the door, and threw myself on the bed with such force I trampolined up twice before flopping face down into the mattress. I stayed there, nose flattened, until I had to take a decent breath of air.

I thought Ethel liked me. I thought she liked having me around, but I could tell by how she talked tonight that she wanted me out. I probably wasn't doing enough work around the place or maybe I ate too much Crunch 'n Munch or maybe she thought that I'd tell people that she ate a whole plastic tubful of ice cream plus cookies during a one-hour TV show.

I felt a terrible pressure in my eyes like they damned back gallons of tears. I started to cry, slowly at first, like I'd forgotten how, but then gushing like a broken water main. I didn't think I could cry so much, that anyone could cry so much. Nothing would be left in my body. I'd dry up like a prune or a raisin. Snot ran down my face and I didn't even wipe it away.

I cried and cried until I was so plugged up, I couldn't breathe. I sat up and sucked air in through my mouth, my lungs on fire. I started wheezing. Someone knocked at a door far away, maybe the house next door, maybe down the street. Death was coming for me right there in that locked room. Things started getting dark around the edges, like an eclipse blackening the day.

Right before I was sure I'd pass out, Ethel burst into the room with a barbecue skewer in her hand. She tossed it on the floor and stood next to my bed. She put her arm around me and pulled me toward her. She didn't pay any attention to the mess on my face. I could taste snot on my lips. She put her other arm around me and she just held me, murmuring, and I felt my heart slow down its efforts to escape my chest.

I didn't cry anymore. I just sat there and felt my whole body turn to mush, like someone had yanked out my skeleton. Ethel was holding me up, I was sure of it. Without Ethel, I would slide to the floor and ooze right under the bed. After a few minutes Ethel reached over to the nightstand and handed me a wad of tissue. I blew my nose and wiped my face. She released her hold on me and left the room, coming back with a glass of water and a wet washcloth.

She held the water while I leaned back on my hands and drank. Then she wiped my face off with the wet cloth and touched my forehead like she was checking for a fever. "You rest now, you'll feel better when you wake up." After pulling the covers up to my neck, she turned the alarm clock to the wall and plugged in the night light, giving a loud grunt when she straightened up.

My head felt like an overripe cantaloupe split on a rock, but I felt something else too. I felt naked in a lashing rain. Ethel had seen me, the real me, the messy me, the not-so-cool me, the me I usually kept safe far inside my body. I wanted to flash freeze myself and thaw out in another life. I scrunched my body to take up the least amount of space, to make myself invisible. I closed my eyes.

I slept for sixteen hours. Ethel didn't wake me when she left for work in the morning. I dreamed all night, long-running dreams where I saw a woman in the distance and Daddy stood next to me saying, "That's your mama, child," but I could see that it couldn't be my mama. This was one of Daddy's sick jokes. He'd been drinking and was having sport with me. This woman had a long skinny neck like a flamingo, but big fat legs like an elephant, and claws painted red at the end of very short arms. "That's not my mother, that's a goddamn freak," I said, and Daddy said, "She used to be a mighty fine-looking woman, till she had you." I looked down at my hands and my right one held a club, my fingers curled around the base. I started hitting Daddy with that club. He didn't run away, he just kept laughing at me so I hit him harder, then harder still. I just got madder and madder that he wouldn't stop laughing. The club passed through him like I wasn't real to him. Then all of a sudden I heard a crunch and blood started gushing out of his head, like a fountain of blood, and he had stopped laughing. I hit him again and his left arm broke off like a stick of candy. Then I whacked at his right arm and that went flying. I was starting to feel peaceful, like I'd found Jesus, nirvana, and enlightenment all at once. Daddy started to frown. The blood gushing out of his head hadn't slowed down. He hadn't run out of blood yet but he was looking scared. Daddy looked scared, scared of me—I liked that a lot. I wanted to finish him off, bring him down. I swung again, this time at his midsection. I knocked a hole clear through him, opening him up like a window. As I bent down to look through the window, he reached toward me. I took the club and punched it straight at his chin. His whole face flew apart and then he was gone. Completely gone. I heard police sirens coming. I dropped the club and looked for the woman he said had been Mama but I couldn't see anyone. I felt a pressing pain in my groin.

I awoke in a wet bed. I had peed my own bed. It smelled bad. I took a hot shower, then stripped the bed and sponged down the mattress. I opened the window to dry out the mattress. Though awake, my body moved on automatic pilot while the dream hung on me like a shroud, tripping up my feet and scraping my palm on the window frame. I hoped that Ethel wouldn't notice anything. I thought of making cabbage for dinner, really stinking the place up. I could keep secrets. I knew how to fool people.

I sat down heavily in a kitchen chair, pouring myself a cup of coffee from the pot that Ethel had left for me. There was a cranberry muffin on a yellow plate and a vitamin next to the orange juice. I drank my coffee thinking how nice it was that Ethel had left breakfast for me. I started feeling weepy again, thinking about how nobody had ever made my breakfast. Not my daddy, not Alva, nobody unless you counted the cook at the International House of Pancakes and then he wasn't making them for me but for some faceless diner out there beyond the swinging kitchen doors.

First I piss my bed and now I'm blubbering like a baby over a muffin and a glass of juice. I wasn't myself. I turned my head away when I caught a bit of my reflection in the toaster. If I looked, I'd see a fun-house self of rotten pumpkin softness flowing in all directions like a pus-popped wound. If I could have stepped out of my skin I would have, molted myself straight out of there. Ejected from my body and gone straight through the ceiling to pass as cloud cover. I had a shaky feeling like I'd just missed being killed on the freeway. I started breathing deeply, my hands gripping the table, and focused my eyes on the kitchen clock, a black cat's tail marking the hours, a tiny red wand sweeping the seconds. I held the table till I had no feeling in my hands and my heart had gone to sleep in my chest, then I let go of the table and put my hands on my thighs. There was nothing between me and me. I crossed my feet at the ankles, dropped my head into my neck, and closed my eyes. I imagined myself a turtle. Maybe I fell asleep like that, maybe I entered some state of alternative consciousness, but an hour passed before I opened my eyes.

I ate my muffin and drank my now cold coffee and the room-temperature orange juice. Ethel would be home in a few hours and I wanted dinner ready when she walked in the front door. I wanted to please her.

That night, after a dinner of meat loaf, garlic bread, endive salad, and apple pie, Ethel and I again planted ourselves on the sofa with the *TV Guide* and the remote control between us. "We watch too much TV, Ethel. We ought to go for walks after dinner."

"You're right, child, but I hate the staring."

"We'll go after dark, not many people out then."

"Aren't you worried about the criminal element?" Ethel liked to watch those shows where you get to help catch killers by calling in to an 800 number.

"You can always roll over on them."

Ethel flicked a paper clip at me. "How amusing."

"What's the first memory you ever had, Ethel?"

"When I was baptized. I was about four years old. My daddy was a Lutheran but not much of one and he didn't want me getting wet in the church, that's how he said it."

"But you did get baptized."

"Mother wore him down. She was a flintstone of woman, never weakened that I could see. He'd finally give in to her, and she would sit in his lap and brush his hair back with her hand and give him this look."

I said, "He liked that look."

"He loved that look. As a kid I only knew that I was never so outside as when she gave that look. Now, of course, I know what all that meant—sex, of course."

"Was your mother good to you?"

"She was, except I always disappointed her because I was always too fat. She'd take me to the Chubby Department. That's what she called it. The dresses would always have stripes going downward and they came in about a million colors. I hate that word 'always,' but if I had to pick one word to describe my life, it would be 'always.'"

I knew how "always" could mark your life.

"What's your first memory, Chloe?"

I told Ethel about being in the bathtub with nothing on but my T-shirt. I was about three and I was thinking how funny it was to be sitting in a tub full of water, more water pouring out of the spigot and me just wearing a T-shirt. I was watching the water slosh up to the top of my thighs and waiting for the T-shirt to get wet, when Mama suddenly ripped the T-shirt right off me, real hard. I felt the shirt drag my ears as she pulled and she had an angry look on her face. I didn't feel so cute anymore, things didn't seem funny anymore.

"You poor child," Ethel said while wiping at her eyes with a tissue.

I wondered for a minute who the poor child was, then I realized she meant me. I eased into the sympathy I could feel coming from Ethel like sun on a cool day. My body warmed as I watched her ball up a bit of Kleenex as she spoke. "Nothing sadder than a motherless child."

I felt sadness coming on me like a blow. I ducked, I sprang off the sofa announcing that I wanted some ice cream, did she?

"Butter brickle, chocolate sauce, whipped cream, and three cherries on top," Ethel sniffled.

I didn't wait for the ice cream to soften. I took the metal scoop and went at it like I had a jackhammer. Ethel hadn't acted any different toward me since last night that I'd noticed, and I'd had my antennae up and in full rotation. But I just couldn't take any more talking about my mother.

Tuesday came and went but no Zena. Ethel stood at the gate and waited but she wasn't on the plane. Ethel didn't seem surprised, just shrugged when she told me of the no-show. That night I kept waking up expecting to see Zena standing over me like some spiritual visitation, saying that she had missed her plane. Ethel went on as if Zena had never called.

"Chloe, how would you like to go to a meeting of Other Friends with me?"

"What's Other Friends?"

"This little group of people who aren't quite like everyone else. You know, the kind that defy the law of average."

I figured Other Friends to be a bunch of fat people.

"Will I fit in?" Maybe I could pad myself up a little with a few pillows and four or five malteds.

"Like tea in a tea ball." Ethel scratched at the side of her neck. I watched her finger burrow into a roll of flesh. I sucked in my stomach. Maybe I had been putting on a few pounds.

"The meeting starts at eight P.M." Ethel threw a dish towel at me. "Let's get these dishes done."

We pulled into an industrial park and wended our way to Building H where Ethel parked next to a minivan with a HONK IF YOU'RE FOR PEACE bumper sticker plastered over the back window.

Room 18 in Building H was open with the light emptying out onto a sidewalk lined with card tables. We went up to the first one and signed in, and at the next table we put on our name tags. On the third table a stack of neatly typed agendas was held down with a rock, a TAKE ONE sign taped to the table. Ethel nudged me past the last table.

"What's that one for?" I asked.

"Special interests." Ethel took my arm and pulled me inside.

I took in a quick view of the room. It was a sideshow looking for a carnival barker. One man looked fine till he turned toward me. One side of his face had been burned and settled in striated scars, one eye hooded shut. A woman taller than a giraffe and a man smaller than a two-year-old stood talking, the woman's head bent down at an awkward angle. I wanted to stare at each one of them and I wanted never to see them again. I wanted to ask each of them how they had come to be that way. I wanted to leave the room.

Ethel started introducing me and nobody seemed surprised that I was there. I wanted someone, anyone, to comment on my normality, the oddity of me being there among all of them. But they all smiled and shook my hand and looked me right in the eye. I smiled back at them, willing them to see me, really see me and know that I wasn't like them. One by one, they listened to Ethel tell the story of how her niece, Zena, had met me on the bus and taken me home to her. How Zena had gone to New York and I was staying on. She told them that I was a big help to her and good company. I just nodded and smiled. Any politeness that I picked up in my life steadied me through the rest of the evening. One man had hands so twisted that he could only hold a pair of pincers using both hands. He used those pincers to bring a cup of punch to his mouth. He took little sips.

The meeting began. The speaker had what looked like a gigantic rash all over his face and body. He gaveled through the announcements, old business, new business, a picnic on private property, a fund-raiser for Ethical Understanding. The drone settled me into my chair. Ethel proposed a small increase in dues, the man with the pincer hands seconded, the others voted the motion in. I didn't vote. After the business part of the meeting, people started to drift away and finally Ethel nodded me toward the door. Standing outside the car, I stared at my face in the rearview mirror, first one side and then the other. Ethel honked the horn. I climbed into the front seat.

"Why did you take me there?"

"To test your character." Ethel backed out of the parking space without turning her head to look behind her.

"Did I pass?" I was sure that I had. I slipped my thumb under the seat belt that crossed my chest.

"No."

I turned to face her. "What did I do wrong?" I fast-forwarded through the evening and could only see my shining, virtuous self.

"You had no sense of outrage. No feeling for the injustice of it all." Ethel turned the radio on to one of those easy-listening stations. I snapped it right off.

"What was I supposed to do, pump pity for them? I can't help them. I thought I was good, really good." I emphasized "really good."

"You didn't feel for them because you don't feel for yourself. You've got armadillo armor, a safety-glass heart, a Simonized soul."

"Well, you're fucking fat. You jiggle when you walk, your thighs rub raw, and you take up too much damn space in the world."

I expected that remark to drive Ethel straight to Baskin-Robbins for a cardboard tub of Rocky Road but instead she drove home. She said not a word to me all the way back but when she locked up the car, she shook my hand and said that she was happy to meet me. I thought she was nuts, some kind of sugar deprivation in her cells. I had noticed that she hadn't hit the refreshment table at the meeting. My insides were starting to churn. Maybe it was time for me to leave again. I followed Ethel into the house.

"I don't want you to leave." Ethel's voice came from the kitchen. "I like you. You just need a little waking up, and tonight was a start."

I said nothing but walked down the hall to my room and slammed the door shut. I felt more pitiful than anyone with pincer hands or a half-there face. They could avoid mirrors, slouch down, go to their meetings. What did I have? I'd never get my mother back. I'd never be a real child. I'd always be an impostor. I felt like slapping myself across the face. I didn't know why Ethel had taken me there. I walked back to the kitchen.

"Why did you take me there?"

Ethel smiled at me when I came in as if nothing had happened. "Because you need to learn how to be outside yourself as well as inside yourself."

"Meaning?"

"Meaning figure it out for yourself."

"Ethel, you're fucking weird."

She started laughing, jiggling from her chins down to her ankles. "You're catching on, kid."

"Don't take me any more places like that. I don't like how they make me feel."

"Okay, Chloe. You want a glass of wine before beddy time?"

I drank two glasses of wine and went to sleep with my clothes on. Before I fell asleep I imagined myself unscrewing the pincers from the fingers of the man with the twisted hands and twisting back on two new hands, soft, fleshy hands that he used to touch my face like a lover. Then I deflated the six-hundred-and-fifty-pound woman, the one Ethel liked to stand next to, saying that the woman made her look "skinny." Using a pump handle that grew out of her left side, moving it briskly up and down, I watched as she grew smaller. As she became half the woman she had once been, she also grew taller. When the pump handle jammed, I stopped. She looked like any middle-aged woman might leaning over the meat counter to pick out tonight's dinner. Then I shortened the tall woman by placing her in a giant press and pushing until she came in at five feet six inches. I think that's the part where I fell asleep because then I heard a buzzing sound. Someone was about to work on me. I started yelling out, "There's nothing wrong with me, there's nothing wrong with me, there's nothing wrong with me." That's when Ethel turned the light on in my room and asked if I was OK. I must have said something because she shut the light off and I fell back to sleep, finally free of dreams.

At breakfast the next day, I knew I had to apologize to Ethel. "I'm sorry I said you were fat, Ethel."

"But I am fat. I'm just not fucking fat."

That night Ethel and I sat side by side on the sofa and watched *Mildred Pierce* while using up a box of Kleenex between us. I cried because I'd never had a mother and if I had, I never, ever, would have treated her so badly.

"You want Zena to come back?" Ethel and I sat across from each other at the dinner table, the serving dishes forming a hedge between us.

"Sometimes."

"I wasn't all that surprised that she didn't come back when she said she was coming." Ethel flapped the cloth napkin onto her lap. "Zena's not reliable." She squared her julienned carrots.

I wasn't sure where this conversation was going.

"Zena has no more direction than a dust bunny. She'll go whichever way she's swept."

"It didn't seem that way to me. She seemed to be going places." I reached for the gravy bowl to fill the crater I'd made in my mashed potatoes.

"I know, she's always been that way. But it's no more real than her saying she loved you in that note she left."

That remark made me mad. I gave her my deadly-daggers look. I wanted to stab her in that inner tube of an arm and see if she'd take off upward, spiraling as the air hissed out of her. She sat there looking at me like I was a junkyard dog, all worked up over something not worth defending.

I said, "I wasn't born yesterday. I know she doesn't love me."

"The big difference between you and Zena is that she does whatever she feels and you don't do anything you feel."

All I said was "OK." Followed by "Pass the corn."

Winter in Phoenix was like a really good spring in most of the country. I sat on a white plastic lawn chair with my feet up on a side table watching the sidewalk traffic. A kid on a plastic tricycle came barreling along making roaring noises with his voice. Ethel was taking a shower and I was on my second cup of coffee. Two speed-walking ladies passed by and I threw them a quick wave. They continued their ducklike motion down the street. The sky was cloud free, just an ocean of blue, and the temperature a comfortable seventy-three degrees. I could see why old people moved here and set up trailer towns while back in the Snow Belt winter raged. Having the sun out every day and a sky so blue I wanted to drink it in put me in an up mood. I could even think about Alva without feeling I had done something wrong. Maybe I'd had sun deficiency all those years, not enough light in my life, not enough warmth.

Alva always told me, "Chloe, you let people make you look stupid. You believe everything they tell you." Now that was a lie. I didn't believe everything. I just took a little longer to decide what I didn't believe. I'd been thinking about Alva a lot lately. Hearing his voice in my head, as if he were in the room with me. I had been wrong about Alva, he really did say a lot more than the ten or so phrases I had given him credit for. But I supposed if you were to press the words just a little, it would still come down to the same few ideas. And those ideas just weren't mine.

It bothered Alva something terrible when I didn't agree with him. I was never up in his face about it. I'd stay calm as could be and say, "Alva, I just don't see things that way." I might as well have said, "Alva, your mama have any children that weren't brain dead?" Of course, he was subtle, no screaming or yelling for Alva, but he'd criticize something I'd made for dinner or comment on his allergies acting up because of the amount of dust in the house. Or he'd bump into me in the hallway like all of a sudden there wasn't enough room for both of us to pass without him bumping me. The ties that bind were there all right, like piano wire around my neck.

I'm exaggerating. Alva always said that I exaggerated, that I put on just a little, that I could turn a black-and-white television into color just by looking at the screen. Alva said a lot of things.

Ethel told me what she thought straight out even if it made me want to stab holes in her. Alva never really went at anything head on. He was more like a guerrilla fighter—a hit-and-run driver—he never hung around to see the burning village or the wreck. He'd done his part and that was all that mattered.

I'd been trashing Alva lately every time he came to mind, but when Ethel mentioned Alva, I always defended him. I'd say, "Alva was OK, I just wasn't the right woman for him." But in my head I'd think that maybe his mother had been the only right woman for him.

Having sex with Zena was different than sex with Alva. I wouldn't call either experience making love, but at least Zena hadn't rolled over and gone straight to sleep. Maybe women were different than men that way, maybe sex between women was less exhausting than sex between men and women.

Alva wasn't all bad. He'd bring home lottery tickets and talk about all the things he'd buy me if he won. He never said if *we* won, he always said if *he* won. I'd married a man as unlike my father as possible, but in some ways, on some days, I saw Alva as the same man, only a softer version.

Ethel came up behind me. She had a towel wrapped turban-style on her head and she wore a terry cloth bathrobe big enough to hide a family of four. "Chloe, your mouth's hanging open and you'll be drooling any minute now. We got to get to work."

"I'm ready."

Ethel asked, "What were you thinking about?"

"Alva being like my daddy."

"You're tuning in the picture, honey."

"And you're not even dressed yet."

Ethel said, "I'm a natural sort of woman, I can be ready in ten minutes."

I looked at my watch. "That would be nine-thirty-two A.M."

"Time me."

I did and she was ready in ten minutes.

We opened the shop at 10:00 A.M. By 11:30, flowers waiting for delivery were lined up like soldiers one right after the other on the counter.

Ethel handed me the addresses. I opened the drawer to get out the keys for the van and studied the map, figuring out which route would use the least gas, the way Ethel had taught me. I loaded the van, fitting each arrangement in the grid that took up most of the back of the van. After spraying the flowers with a light mist, I turned the key in the ignition and the engine groaned, then turned over.

I liked delivering flowers. I always read the message on the card before I made the delivery. I hated to leave the flowers or the plant with a neighbor, then I couldn't see the surprised looks on the faces of the people when I proffered up my delivery. The fact that they didn't know that I had read the card gave me an inside sense about them. I knew things about them that they didn't know about me. That made me feel safer, like I was a one-way mirror and they were just plain window glass.

Some of those messages took up all the space on that tiny card and some people stuffed two or three into a little envelope and then taped it shut. I kept a roll of tape in the van just for those kind of notes so I could replace the tape after I read the note. But mostly people kept the message short and mushy, using lots of nicknames: pumpkin, sweet-ums, love muffin. I figured some of the people sending the flowers were lying, but most were truthful. I'd never received flowers.

I had three deliveries this morning. At the first one I rang the bell about ten times. I could hear kids hollering around the house and Ernie telling Bert some paper-clip story—that's how loud the TV was. When the door opened, a woman held a baby in her right arm and had her left hand clamped around the wrist of an unrepentant-looking three-year-old. I saw two other kids under the kitchen table where they were putting together a Lego set.

"I have a delivery from Fiona's Flowers."

She put the baby down on the floor. He threw his fat arms around her ankle and started to scream. "Go to your room," she hissed to the toddler, releasing his wrist to give him a push toward his room. One of the kids came out from under the table, a girl with bangs edging into her eyes, and gave the toddler another push. The boy came up behind her, punching her on the arm. The baby began whining at a glass-breaking pitch.

"Something for us, Mom?" the Lego kids said. Their hopeful voices made me wish I did have something for them.

"No, not you two, you have everything, I have nothing."

"You have us, Mom," the boy reminded her with a tone his father might have used.

"No kidding, that's probably why I never win the lottery, I've already been so damn lucky."

I handed her the flowers. She tucked the bouquet under her arm and used one incredibly long manicured nail to rip open the flap on the envelope. She blew out her breath informing the kids that the flowers were from their "can't keep his dick in his pants daddy." I looked at the children. Their faces had closed over like they'd been asked a question they didn't know the answer to. "Am I supposed to tip you?" she asked.

I said no. I didn't really want to stay around any longer than I had to. She told me, "He sends me flowers because I'm having another one. I've got four right now. He don't believe in birth control, says God don't like it. Don't matter what I like." I heard what she was saying, but my heart was with the children. I had seen them close up. They knew about danger. They'd learned to smell it in the air, hair raising up on their arms just a bit, a shakiness beneath the feet like the shadowy rumblings of a geyser about to blow. She closed the door and I remembered that the card had said "God Bless You, honey."

Alva had wanted to have kids, but I kept saying, "Not yet. Pretty soon." I took the Pill religiously. I didn't feel old enough to have kids. Now I was glad not to have any and even gladder that I didn't have to take the Pill anymore since I just wasn't doing anything that could get me that way. I'd be safe.

The second stop was better—a young girl, face glowing, kind of dancing around with the flowers. She gave me a dollar and I smiled. The card said "To my one true love, I'd die for you." Reading the cards gave me jealous fits sometimes. In my life, no one would die for me, they couldn't even stay around long enough to enroll me in kindergarten. If it's a point in Daddy's favor that he kept me around, it's a weak one. He always looked at me like some day I'd be of use, he was sure of that. I guess I disappointed him.

I left the flowers with a next-door neighbor at my last stop. Sometimes people get this hopeful look, thinking the flowers are for them, then find out they belong to someone else. Some folks can get downright ugly when they're asked to keep them until their neighbor comes home. This woman curled her lip so far up that with a good snort she could have sucked her lip right up her nose. I thanked her and told her that the flower shop would call later today to check on the delivery. I said that just in case she had any thoughts about keeping the flowers.

I took the van down to be washed and gassed and then stopped at a Taco Bell for lunch. The high school kids had swarmed in for lunch and I felt achy inside seeing them. They thought they had all the time in the world, that their lives were made of a flexible sort of cast iron, that they could be twisted many ways but still survive anything. Wait till they find out that there's cast iron in the junkyard all rusted up and dented like everything else. I don't think there's anybody around who isn't disappointed in some way at how life has turned out.

Back at the shop, I stayed behind the counter while Ethel went to lunch with a supplier. It was past one and quiet except for a few ladies stopping in on their lunch hour to browse. I sometimes thought of me and Ethel as two maiden aunts, except I was much younger. I felt safe with Ethel. I liked having a routine. It steadied me like the ballast on hot-air balloons.

"I ate like a bird," Ethel whispered to me after the supplier left the shop, "a flock of birds and a swarm of mosquitoes." She started laughing, then belched, and the smell of onions almost wilted the flowers.

"You need a breath mint." I handed her the roll we kept under the counter for such occasions.

"I need a roll of breath mints. I'm a big woman. I do things in a big way."

I couldn't deny it. Ethel did do things in a big way. Everything—eating, laughing, talking—nothing came quietly to her. She once said that people were already looking at her, so she might as well give them something to look at. Her clothes had Crayola color brightness. There was nothing subtle about her, but she had a gentleness, as if she knew enough about pain not to go out of her way to add any more grief to the world.

At night, Ethel would sit down next to me on the sofa and open up two boxes of Cracker Jacks—one for her and one for me—and she'd eat all of hers, then ask if I was done with mine yet. She didn't comment on the show we were watching until the commercial, then she'd ask me what I thought of the story line. Did I buy it or get it or like it? I enjoyed having someone ask my opinion even more than the sweets or the bowls of ice cream. I'd never realized how many opinions I actually had.

Ethel finished up the roll of breath mints, crunching them like chicken bones.

"Ethel, I think we spend entirely too much time watching TV and eating. I've put on five pounds since I've been here."

"I know. I don't really have a glandular problem, I just tell that to people. It's kind of a test. If they look like they don't believe me, then I know one thing about them. I know that they think I am what I am because of my own doing and internal weakness. If they believe me, I know that they'll give me enough space to be me."

I said, "I know about space."

"You don't take up enough space." Ethel had her reading glasses on and dipped her head toward me. I could count five chins and the glasses magnified her blue eyes.

"I will soon if I keep eating like that every night."

"I don't mean that kind of space. I mean your *being* doesn't take up enough space."

I looked at Ethel. I didn't quite get what she was saying.

"You're entitled to more than you're taking. Think it over."

I knew what she meant, but knowing made me feel like I was stuck atop a Ferris wheel in a high wind, the basket swaying back and forth.

Chapter Ten

Most of my daddy's girlfriends paid no mind to me at all. I was just there, like cheap furniture. Most of what I know I learned by watching. Like a dog will howl and horses move around a corral right before a tornado, I have that sense of things about to happen. Since I was so seldom spoken to, words have not confused my thinking. What I know, I know without sound, like a goldfish can tell when you're watching him swim around in his bowl even if you're looking in from another room. Try it someday, you will see this is true.

The first time that Daddy and I lived in a regular house, I was eleven. It was just past the Fourth of July. Daddy had been seeing a woman named Loretta who had red hair and eyes greener than the first blades of spring grass. We moved into her little white house which sat right next to another little white house with a narrow strip of gravel between them. I had my own room with a window that looked out onto the place next door. The same man owned both houses. His name was Mr. Canson and he had known Loretta from back when her husband had been alive.

Daddy started to settle down a little. Seed catalogues came in the mail and he'd talk about putting a garden in the back, though I

liked things the way they were: knee-high grass, wildflowers, lots
of bugs.

Daddy met Loretta at the Feed Bag Diner. She had stayed with
us nights off and on at the motel, but she finally talked Daddy into
coming back to her house. I think Daddy had a feeling for Loretta
that he didn't get for most women.

"This is your room, kid."

"Thank you, Miss Loretta."

"It ain't much but it's yours."

"I never had my own room before. I'll take real good care of it."

I wanted Loretta to leave so that I could be alone in my room.

She said, "Lots of kids don't have their own rooms."

I looked around the room. The walls were white and in the corner of the room was a small bed with a nubby brown blanket.
There was a tall dresser and a huge upholstered chair in a nasty
color of green. A lamp with a clear glass globe sat on the dresser,
and overhead a ceiling light glowed down making a circle of light
in the center of the room.

"Shut the lights off when you don't need 'em. I sold all my electrical stock."

I didn't understand what she meant by selling all her electrical
stock. I looked at her and she gave me a kind of crooked grin and I
knew she was joking. "Yes ma'am," I said.

"You know, you're awful polite for a child without a mama."

"Thank you."

Loretta looked disappointed, as if she wanted something else
from me. For myself, I had learned that "yes ma'am," "no sir,"
"please," and "thank you" were ways of keeping myself safe and
not drawing unfavorable attention. Good manners had no value to
me beyond that.

After Loretta left, I emptied out my paper sack full of clothes,
putting everything neatly away. Even if I put my underwear and
pajamas in separate drawers, I still had three empty drawers full of
nothing but air and possibility.

I can't explain exactly what hold Loretta had over Daddy. He
looked at her the way a pet dog looks when you have a doggie treat

in your hand—full of interest and intelligence. Whatever she had, Daddy wanted. But she didn't need him the way the other women had. Like she knew something he didn't, and she wasn't going to tell him.

The week before school started, Loretta took me down to Kmart and bought me three new dresses, five pairs of underwear, and a plastic bag full of white socks. After that we went to the shoe store where you could look at your feet through a machine and see all the bones in your foot like you were a ghost. She bought me a new pair of brown shoes and a bottle of polish. "Only wear these to school. No stepping in puddles and don't drag your feet when you're on the playground. And polish them every Sunday night."

I had heard Loretta tell Daddy she needed money to get me things and she had stood over him when he signed my school papers. She told him that as long as we were living with her, she "didn't want no goddamn truant brat dressed like a hobo giving her a bad name." He gave her the money and told her to save a little to get something for herself. He said, "The kid don't need much. Don't go spoiling her."

Daddy didn't like it when his girlfriends paid attention to me. Before this, most of them had only noticed me when they wanted something, like a beer. One of them, Desiree—Desire is what Daddy called her—told him he ought to put me in an orphanage or sell me to somebody now that I was getting old enough to do "meaningful work." Desiree wasn't with us very long. She stole money from Daddy and he threw her out right into the motel parking lot and then tossed her suitcase into the Dumpster out front.

On my first day of school Loretta, who didn't like to get up before eleven and cursed the birds for being too damn noisy, was cooking me eggs and toast.

"I can't do this every day, but the first day of anything is special, even prison I suppose."

Loretta being nice made me feel good, but I kept my eye on Daddy, because I knew that he wanted her to like him better. When he thought I was getting a little too big for my britches, he would say to me, "Now, Chloe, I wouldn't want to see you wind up in one of them state institutions. They got all kinds, you know, for the not too bright, for the crazier than a loon, for the ones who got nobody else, for the criminals—all kinds of places."

So I thanked Loretta and kept my room tidy and brought home my school papers to show her. She tossed them out after she looked at them, but she said, "You're an OK kid." I didn't show the papers to Daddy.

At school I towered over the other kids and they laughed at things I didn't think were funny. I was just more serious, I guess. I wanted to learn everything and I wanted to learn everything just right. My clothes were new and clean and Loretta insisted that I take a bath every night and that meant washing my hair every other night.

Loretta let me look through what she called her junk jewelry drawer and gave me two sparkly rings that the girls at school kept begging to borrow and a necklace that I told everyone was made of real gold. I said I had found it in a motel room in East Tulsa. I picked a faraway place so they would be more likely to believe me. Most of them had never even left town, so once they found out all the places I'd been and heard about all the things I said I'd seen, I became like a peacock in a neighborhood of sparrows.

I knew more about sex than these kids did, even the ones that came in from the farms. I suppose that helped me keep my place in school—the things I knew, and the information I was willing to share. To this day, I prize knowledge. The more I know, the safer I'll be.

While the boys played baseball or practiced spitting, the girls usually knotted into small groups of two or three. I had managed to draw ten or so girls together. The subject was sex. I told all I knew. I stood in the center surrounded by kids like a full moon attended by a sky full of stars.

"Why do men like to do it so much?" My mother's always telling my father that he's acting like an animal." The girl asking the question had short blonde hair and dark brown eyes. I had heard one of the kids say that everybody thought her real dad was a gypsy.

"Men can't help themselves." I had just explained to the girls what kinds of things men do to women to make them want it, the touching and kissing and rubbing and all. I knew so much because Daddy and his girlfriends had never much cared whether I was really asleep or not, and lots of times I hadn't been.

"Do women need it?" I couldn't place the voice with a girl.

"Not the way men do." I separated each word, adding a meaningful shake of my head.

"Does it hurt?" The question came from a little girl, the one they called Shrimp. She squeezed her legs together.

"Nah, but they moan like it's killing them."

"Did you ever see your parents doing it?" challenged Martha, a girl whose mother matched the barrettes in her hair to the color of her dress.

My "yes" rang with arrogance. Hands flew to open mouths. I added that it wasn't a pretty sight, not like in those romance novels, all nice and neat. No, it was a messy business and I was in no hurry to have any of it myself.

The recess bell rang us in and I could feel the looks as I sauntered into line. I knew I could trade on my fame. Being visible felt good. I told everyone at school, including my teacher, that Loretta and Daddy were married, though I don't think my teacher, Miss Elliot, believed me. She patted me on the head, told me "that's nice dear," and sent me back to my seat. So when the kids saw me walking with Loretta and Daddy downtown, I knew what they were thinking. And I had given them those thoughts.

Although I played with kids on the playground and I had become an expert of sorts, I wasn't invited to their homes or to their birthday parties. But still I was happier than I'd ever been before. I did my homework, raised my hand right up, not waving it all over the place like I was swatting at a mosquito. I erased neatly and, if there was any extra work to be done, I did it. By the end of the year, I received A's in all my subjects. Loretta bought me a hot fudge sundae to celebrate. Daddy just grunted.

Daddy worked steady now at the steel mill. He'd come home smelling like metal and always seemed to have that smell about him even when he took his one-week vacation and sat in the back-yard drinking beer, saying he didn't want to go anywhere because he'd seen enough of the open road.

Loretta changed shifts and now worked the lunch and early evening crowd at the diner. She went to work about ten-thirty in the morning and came home about seven-thirty at night. She usually left something for me to heat up for dinner. I didn't like those dinners with Daddy. We ate in silence, and when we were done he walked away from the table as if he had eaten alone. I'd clean up knowing that Loretta would be tired when she got home.

"I'm home," Loretta yelled out, letting the screen door slam behind her. "My dogs are killing me, kid."

"You want me to rub them?" Loretta had told me that I had magic hands and that after a hot soak, nothing could bring her tootsies back to life like a foot massage with peppermint lotion by yours truly.

"I do, sugar. Why, after you're done with my feet, I feel like dancing." She'd sit down at the kitchen table and I'd draw a basin of warm water. While her feet soaked, she'd drink a soda and tell me some story about a customer. Then I'd rub her feet while she read the paper. Daddy was usually in bed by then because he worked the early shift at the mill. If he didn't have work the next day, he would stand at the top of the stairs and yell, "Loretta, get up here right now, I need something."

Daddy had changed since meeting Loretta. He still didn't pay me much mind, but he didn't get mad the way he used to. The only time that I think he really saw me was when Loretta and I were together in some way like talking or Loretta was combing my hair, and then his eyes would skim over me to reach Loretta. Some kids will do all kinds of crazy things to get attention, but I wasn't that kind. For Daddy, I existed only as an extension of Loretta, like a third arm, which was better than getting hit.

Daddy especially talked to Loretta when he'd had some beer. His daddy had sold life insurance and kept his tool bench cleaner than an operating room. My daddy had been the youngest of six boys, "runt" was what they called him. The brothers grew up to play football and pick fights, but when it came to my daddy all the size seemed to be gone and he came out short and lean. His hair was dark instead of blonde like the others and there had been some nasty fights between his parents on that subject. Daddy thought that maybe he looked so different because he hadn't had the same father. I thought about the blonde girl with the brown eyes, the one with the gypsy father.

There were times when I hated Daddy. It's hard to hate somebody you're supposed to love, but it's even harder to have somebody not love you when he's supposed to. What kind of person are you, if nobody loves you?

That September when I would enter fifth grade, Loretta threw Daddy out for turning so jealous that he almost cost her job, coming round to the diner to check on her. We left town then with sixty bucks of Loretta's money. Loretta had a black eye and I didn't go back to school until December.

Chapter Eleven

My legs woke me up twitching like a dog having a dream. I felt agitated like I had to move, and if I didn't, my body would just start doing a St. Vitus dance and I wouldn't be able to stop. I put on my shoes and went outside. I started walking down the streets, looking into the brightly lit front windows of other people's lives.

In one house, the kitchen was flooded with light, while the other rooms rested in darkness. A woman stood at the kitchen sink, the lines of her face starkly shown by the fluorescent tube overhead, her motions practiced as she washed up the dinner dishes. Her ragdoll movements made me think of myself and the days I had left behind. Part of me wanted to knock on her front door and offer to finish up for her while she sat down in the living room with her feet up. But another part of me, a stronger part, wanted to stay away from her as if she were a leper or a carrier of the plague.

A teenage boy sat at his desk in front of a window with beer cans stacked pyramid-style, his head bent over an open book. Had he drunk all that beer or was the pyramid a declaration of a future goal? People began to draw the drapes. Porch lights came on. The night was chilly and plumes of chimney smoke bloomed into the night sky. I walked until my jumpiness settled into weariness, long past the time when anyone was on the street.

Something was changing in me. I kept saying things just as soon as they came into my head. Sometimes I said stupid things, as if I had lost some critical edge, and then I'd laugh. Other people would laugh too. Then I'd laugh some more. Maybe I was losing my mind. It hadn't been an unpleasant experience so far. I thought maybe something was growing on my brain like mold on cheese and pretty soon I'd start baying at the moon.

Alva had sent me to a shrink. He said that I was just moping around, and "after all, it's in my benefit package, ain't it?" Talking to somebody who had to listen to you and wouldn't burden you with their problems in a tit-for-tat fashion was a real luxury. Alva tried to find out what we talked about. He figured he would get a report on me since, after all, his benefits were paying for the talking.

He came with me once. Started asking her questions. She kept telling him that he would have to ask me. "She don't tell me nothing," he said to her in an aggrieved tone.

"Then I guess that's what she wants you to know."

He didn't like that. Alva figured most things could be fixed by not thinking about them. Keeping busy. "Thinking don't change nothing. Only doing changes things." Alva was right. And I did something. I left him.

I'm not faulting Alva. Crazy people can be hard to live with and I have no doubt that I was crazy there for a while. Always sitting around remembering, swamping myself in the past. Some nights, there wouldn't be any dinner when he came home. At first he said that everyone had bad days, but after a while he just lost patience with me. He said that life was a matter of will power and unless a truck ran you over, you ought to just pull yourself up by your bootstraps.

Part of my trouble with Alva was that I had told him too much about myself. I hadn't left any mystery. I usually lied to men about who I was and where I came from. I think they liked it better that way. They seemed happier not knowing. With Alva, I told him about my mama leaving and my daddy dragging me across the country and me not having any roots to speak of until those high school years with my aunt Dolly but by then my insides were cast. The best, truest part of the self is in the very middle, the part that lives first and runs the show forever and ever. It's what makes the real you, not the shell that everyone sees, and I firmly believe that self formed the day Mama left me.

I think that my shrink liked me, but if I had told her about my leaving Alva, she probably wouldn't like me anymore. When I didn't show up for my next appointment, did she call the house? She was my very first shrink, so I don't know, but I'm hoping she didn't. I can imagine the kind of spin that Alva would put on things. Maybe she will try to help *him* now by giving him a discount rate or maybe telling him everything she knows about me.

She asked me once if I trusted her. I told her that I didn't know. I knew that she wanted me to say yes. If I didn't trust her, it had more to do with me than with her, except for the fact that she had a funny way of turning a phrase. She once told me that she thought it was very easy for people, both men and women, to fall in love with me. I suppose I looked shocked. She added, leaning forward in her chair, that love didn't have to be sexualized. She said the strangest things. Maybe she was in love with me or maybe I was in love with her and that's why I didn't go back to her and why I left home. It was just one more thing that I couldn't stop thinking about.

I stopped at the quik-mart on the way back home and called Alva at work. That way he wouldn't go sobbing on me with the guys hanging around.

"I'd like to speak to Alva Edward Herson."

It took him a few minutes to get to the phone and I kept rearranging my quarters on the scummy metal shelf of the pay phone booth and reading about whom to call for a hot time.

"Hello."

"Alva, it's me."

His words tumbled out with a thickness that made me nervous. "You all right? Where are you? When you coming back?"

"Who's the woman, Alva?"

"You called the house?"

I repeated, "Who's the woman, Alva?"

"I been working overtime, double shifts. That was the sitter. Their mom has gone to a fellowship meeting out in the woods somewhere. I got the kids."

"Why'd you watch me all the time, Alva?"

"I didn't want you to leave me."

A long silence stretched out between us.

The operator's voice came in, telling me to put more money in. I plugged the quarters into the phone and listened to the clink as each coin hit home.

"I want you to come back home. I won't watch you no more."

"I don't think I can do that," I said.

"At least come back so that we can talk a little." A slight whine had come into his voice.

"I'll think about it." I scratched at the gummy surface of the shelf with my thumbnail, then wiped my finger off on my jeans in disgust.

Alva talked for a while about all the good times that we had had together. I didn't remember most of them. When the operator cut in again to niggle me for quarters, I hung up.

At first leaving Alva had made me feel new again, like a snake shedding a skin. A starting-over kind of thing, fresh slate, all that stuff that people promise when they say that they forgive you but they don't really. I don't think anyone really forgives anyone else. That's probably the biggest lie we tell ourselves. When we say we forgive but can't forget, what are we really saying? Forgiving involves forgetting and forgetting is just too much to expect from such slowly evolving creatures as ourselves. I read once of the idea that we live many lifetimes and in each one we move toward what we're really supposed to be. I think maybe the problem with me and Alva was that I was on Life Six and he was only on Life Two. Course those numbers change depending on the kind of day I'm having. Sometimes I feel like I'm just starting out and haven't learned a damn thing, then other days I think that if I pick up one more little bit of wisdom I'll just explode with the holding of it all.

But I was missing Alva. I missed his slow steadiness acting as a wind drag on my life, the heft of his body paperweighting me to the world, the way I'd slow down my words to watch the creasing of his eyes when he smiled. But I wasn't about to go back. This was just weakness on my part. I could talk myself out of this. When I first met Alva, I didn't talk much about myself. Most of what I told him wasn't true, just stuff I said because I wanted him to like me. I didn't want him to know how different I was.

I wanted to be just like Alva when I met him. He made me feel safe. I didn't want him to feel sorry for me like he was rescuing a stray. And I didn't want him to think that my true life had made me crazy, which is what he accused me of being right before I left. I had by then told him about the unspoken parts of my life, having sunk into a morass of moodiness, after which he had taken to scanning the house like one of those dogs that sniff out dope before he went much past the front door.

I don't know when feeling safe with Alva went into feeling suffocated as if he had started to sit on me so that I flattened into the earth and could hardly get up. He said that he wasn't doing that, but I felt like he was. Alva wanted to be too close, I couldn't bear that feeling anymore, and so I left.

It didn't help that Alva had two kids from his first marriage. They came around every other weekend, muddying up the waters between us. His first wife had gone to Jesus on him and wouldn't allow anything in the house that didn't smack of the Lord and righteous ways and her path was a mighty narrow one. Alva came home one day and found that Tess had poured all his beer down the sink and trashed all the videos that weren't G-rated including *The Wizard of Oz*. She had tossed that one out first, saying movies about witches were the devil's work, even if the witch melted, and besides there weren't any good witches so Glinda was a lie.

She insisted that the whole family go to church on Wednesday night and all day Sunday. What most people would see as poor taste or bad judgment Tess saw as part of a Master Plan for the evilification of the world. Alva went along for a while, drinking his beer at lunch and attending church regular, but then the kids started gnawing away at themselves thinking they had sinned so much in one day that they were damned for sure. They had no faith in the caretaking powers of the Lord, having watched their mother unhinge like a bad door in a hard wind. She got worse and worse until finally she lost it right there in the middle of Woolworth's and started talking to a bin of big vinyl beach balls and then crying her eyes out when none of those "people" would listen to her. Tess spent some time away at a hospital, and when she came home, in one hand she had her release papers and in the other hand the divorce papers. She handed both of them to Alva.

He wanted the kids full time, but she had straightened out enough to get the kids. Alva called them practically every day, expecting that at any minute Tess would fly apart, but she surprised him by keeping herself together enough to get by.

But when the kids visited, they made me out to be a home wrecker though I hadn't even met Alva until after the divorce was official. Two girls, one seven and one twelve, they glommed onto Alva the minute they hit the front door and didn't leave us alone, not even at night, laying claim to horrible nightmares that I'm sure they had spent the previous week concocting. They were really good at it. When the kids finally left on Sunday night, Alva felt full of guilt and the kind of thinking that said he should try harder.

He said, "I should have seen it coming."

I answered, "Who could have seen it? There's no preparing for that kind of thing. It's like an unknown cosmic force." I started to rub his back. He shrugged me off.

"I didn't pay enough attention to her."

I argued, "It's a disease, like polio. None of it is your fault."

Alva insisted on taking his share of the blame. "I shoulda gone to church when she first asked me so I coulda kept a handle on this thing. We shoulda gone out together more. I shoulda . . ."

"Shoulda, coulda, woulda—there's no changing what's gone before." I rested my hand on his knee. He left it there.

"Maybe I should try to get the kids more often." His face brightened at the idea.

"Your kids hate me." I pulled my hand off his knee.

"They do not. They just miss their mother. You could be a little friendlier." He came down hard on the word "friendlier."

"Friendlier? I do just about every damn thing they ask me to do, from helping with their homework to sewing buttons on their clothes, and not once has either of them said 'thank you' to me."

"They're just kids," Alva said as if being kids were some kind of universal explanation for rudeness.

"And I'm just your wife," I said and stood up.

"Take it easy." Alva was using his smoothing-things-over voice.

"Maybe you and Tess ought to be back together for the sake of your little darlings." I looked straight at him.

"Don't go getting snotty on me." Alva's voice had risen and I knew that I was getting to him.

I walked out, just not wanting to be in that room anymore. I stood in the kitchen and lit matches, watching them burn down to my fingertips before I flipped them into the sink. I went through about six packs of matches waiting for Alva to come into the kitchen, but he didn't. I rinsed the burnt matches into the sink strainer and left them there.

Alva and I didn't speak for a few days and then things just changed back to normal with nobody actually saying anything about the kids. It was kind of like a playing card with the two of spades on one side and a picture of a naked woman on the other. Life just flipped right over and the other side was not to be seen.

Alva didn't want to talk most of the time, and when he did want to talk, I didn't want to hear what he had to say. We never both wanted the same thing at the same time. We were like two trains on one track, approaching from opposite directions. It was only a matter of time before the crash.

I shouldn't have married Alva, but to put things in their plainest view, I'd never had anybody pay much attention to me and when Alva took on about me, I couldn't resist. My neediness, like a sponge, took all that loving in. He kissed and hugged me and told me I was beautiful and smart and that I made him laugh. He made me feel so good about myself that I would have walked through fire for that man, at least in the beginning. Slowly, though, it had changed. My life with him had become instead a bed of nails.

I lasted five years. The girls eventually slowed down their campaign to break us up, but the damage had been done. Tess married a salesman who wasn't home much but made a good buck and bought those girls everything they asked for, which made Alva jealous. "Daddy," they said in those little-girl voices they used on him. "Frank bought us new bikes, but he wouldn't take us to the movies more than once on the weekend. Will you take us, Daddy? Twice?"

And Alva would.

He'd insist that I come along. I'd sit there on the end with Alva sandwiched between the girls, their bodies turned toward him, their heads bobbing comments and murmuring in soft girlish voices. I felt like I shouldn't be sitting there. I felt like an intruder, a voyeur, someone who just didn't belong. I hated that feeling. It was too familiar, filled with too much history. Like a shipwreck being raised, lots more came up than just that feeling of not belonging. Heavy, dark, glutton servings of grief, clotting up my throat, ragging my breath, making me feel smaller than my size. The more that came up, the smaller I became, as if the very thing dwarfed me with the presence of my past. What I did then was get up and walk out. They'd come out of the movie holding hands and act surprised to see me sitting in the lobby. They would ask, "What happened to you?" I'd tell them that I had left right at the end of the movie to use the bathroom. No one remembered otherwise.

I never stopped thinking. I couldn't just say, "Well, that's how things are." I have never been good at accepting things. Thinking, remembering, and feeling are my problem areas, like some people can't resist chocolate or slimy men. Sometimes the remembering and feeling became so strong that I couldn't think, and I wasn't myself anymore, and that scared me. I was pure feeling. Some days, I became a receptor for everyone out there sending messages.

I knew things I didn't want to know. I wanted to become blind and mute just to find peace.

I wondered how sad my leaving had made Alva feel. I figured he'd miss the cooking and cleaning, the bill paying and the grocery shopping. I guessed he'd miss me lots. Kind of like having to do without water or electricity. You take those things so much for granted. You don't realize how many times a day you turn on a faucet expecting water or flick on the lights expecting to have darkness chased away or turn a knob so the radio blasts into sound. But when it's not there, you feel surprised, off balance, you lean back a little to steady yourself. Was that how he felt? Once we married, he never said he loved me except during his orgasm when he'd cry "Jesus Christ, I love you." Then I was never sure if it was me or Jesus Christ he was loving. I know why I married Alva. I married him because he was steady. That's also why I left him. Steady became stuffy. Peaceful turned passive. Virtue turned into vice.

I needed the steadiness and peace at first. Made me feel like the world was a more manageable place. But after a while, things that he said were for my own good just didn't feel good to me. Like he didn't want me to go out after dark, said the world was too full of crazy people. We went out together sometimes but mostly to bars where they played country-and-western music. Alva liked to ooze across the dance floor with me plastered to him tighter than wet clothes, my face pressed into his shoulder so that I practically suffocated on his Aqua Velva cologne.

Alva liked to talk about the importance of "a man planting his seed," like every man was Johnny Appleseed. I kept telling him he already had two saplings and what was his rush. Every day I swallowed a birth control pill along with my vitamin. Maybe if I had kids then someday I'd just up and leave them the way Mama had left me. And that would make me a really bad person. Leaving your husband was not nearly as bad—like homicide, it could sometimes be justifiable.

C h a p t e r   T w e l v e

Growing up, my body turned on me. There was nothing I could do to stop what was happening. I tried. I slept on my chest every night hoping that my breasts would flatten out, but they only swelled as if someone inside were pumping me up like a rubber raft. I counted the hairs that appeared between my legs and pulled every third one out. The pleasure I felt at my daring seemed dangerous to me. My jeans grew tighter around my hips and I knew that I could no longer be mistaken for a boy at ten feet. I felt exposed like a faker whose real identity becomes known on *To Tell the Truth*. My future was laid out before me like a Polaroid photo slipping into color right before my eyes. Being seen so clearly as female made me feel like a deer caught in the car headlights.

I felt myself to be a changeling and I slipped out of my own grasp at every turn. Sometimes I would repeat "me, me, me" for several minutes as if it were an incantation capable of summoning up the one I wanted to be.

I spun stories hoping the real me would come forward and claim me. I didn't look like Daddy on the outside and could find no common ground between us. Perhaps I had been kidnapped from a wealthy family, and this man who called himself my father and his now long-gone accomplices had not been able to get the ransom. I hadn't been killed because Daddy was a kidnapper, not a murderer, plus it all happened when I was a small child and couldn't testify against anyone. It seemed a possibility to me.

One rainy Saturday, after walking into town through a fine mist, I went to the library and paper-toweled my hair dry in the bathroom. Then I walked softly into the reference section where the slightest cough sounded like an explosion. I sat down with the books, volumes one and two of *Unsolved Kidnappings*. I started with the year that I was born and went forward until I was six and capable of memory. The hiss of the radiators and the scraping of the chair legs on the industrial carpet were the only sounds I could hear as I read page after page. I never found myself that way, although it was always possible that some other child's body had been found and claimed as mine. A body rotted away in some ditch, turgid with death, my true family thinking I was dead while the dead child's family still lived with the unknown. I could even be from Mars, sent down to research Earth people by being one of them.

I finished late in the afternoon. My hair had dried and I could smell gum on someone's breath. My stomach growled. I had filled my head with stories of missing people, their lives hung out like question marks. I felt like one of those people even if I couldn't find myself in a book.

The rain had stopped. The downtown was starting to empty. I jaywalked across the street to W. T. Grant's department store, where I bought a bag of popcorn and started walking home. I knew now that more businessmen disappeared than children and more criminals vanished than businessmen. A few women never came home from shopping. The finger of suspicion always pointed toward a husband if they had one, or a boyfriend if he seemed the jealous type.

I ate my popcorn a kernel at a time and thought about those missing kids. Did they know they were missing and people were looking for them? I knew they all couldn't be alive, but I wanted to find one of them. The streets were full of people coming out of their houses because the rain had let up. Kids my own age caught my eye and if they had an adult with them I'd look for a family resemblance between them. All the way home, I stared at people so hard that some of them stared back in the rudest way.

When I got back to our motel room, I had a terrible thirst from all that popcorn and felt myself sinking into a tar pit of a mood. I stood in front of the bathroom mirror, wiping away the water spots with the sleeve of my shirt. I stared at myself. My face fascinated me. I practiced different expressions to see how they looked on me. I did all the standards—surprise, shock, grief, anger, joy—and my favorite, mysterious. I already felt that no one knew me and that made mysterious no effort at all. People saw me but they didn't see me. They only saw what I allowed them to see. The less people knew about me, the safer I felt. But my safety came with a deep sadness. After a while my sadness felt safe. It had an easy familiarity, like a recurring disease whose course we know but can't alter.

Much of the time when not jacketed in sadness, I'd feel like I was on a roller coaster ride with no one at the controls. Daddy would pick up and decide to move on but I no more understood why he behaved the way he did than I understood why I'd get so moody one minute and the next feel like giggling.

I prayed for miracles—small miracles, like quarters left in the coin return of a telephone, a boy smiling at me, me winning a contest at school for best picture or best speech. I prayed for big miracles, like Daddy starting to see me for being a person and not just luggage with legs. I prayed for the impossible, Mama coming for me. Tom and baby Lucy had to be straight out of the way. If she found me again, I didn't want to share her. But my life was without miracles. Sometimes, though, I'd catch a sliver of light, a word of praise from a teacher. Suddenly I'd understand a wedge of truth and I'd use that wedge to prop open the door to the room where I liked to keep my secret self.

I never wrote in diaries. Daddy would have read them. As I became older he became suspicious of me in small ways. Maybe he knew that I was stealing from him, pocket change, and collecting it until I'd have enough to turn it into folding money that I kept with me always, stuck under the inside flap of my shoe. I slept with my shoes under my pillow.

Maybe my body made him nervous. I'd catch him looking at me

when he thought I was staring out the window into yet another motel parking lot or at some empty piece of road unraveling in front
of us as the car moved us toward a place we'd never been before. I
should have sensed that change was on the way. But my new body
had demagnetized my true north so I was not ready when the time
came and my life became a mean trick of Fifty-Two Pick-Up.

Chapter Thirteen

Ethel was fat because she ate more than any human being that I have ever seen. When I started living with her that was all I could see, how much she ate and how all that fat robed her body like a pear dipped in chocolate again and again until there was more chocolate than pear. There was more fat than there was Ethel, or at least that's what I thought in the beginning.

"Yes, Chloe, this is my third helping, using the biggest spoon in the kitchen, of this delicious sausage stuffing."

I'd smile, but living with Ethel I'd learned to take what I wanted first, otherwise I might starve. After eating, she'd get that stupefied look that puppies get after filling their bellies at the chow bowl, just before they roll on their backs so satisfied that they drop right off to sleep. Food didn't satisfy me that way, but then neither did sex. At least not sex with Alva. My mind wandered when Alva was on top of me. I'd think about how I ought to use lemon oil on the furniture and not that spray stuff that turned wood furniture into plastic after ten years of continuous use. Sometimes I'd actually think about Alva, about how heavy he felt upon my body, like the stone they say covered the opening to the cave where Jesus' body lay until he was resurrected. Getting away from Alva had been a kind of resurrection for me. I felt lighter living without Alva, though some days

I'll admit to missing him the way you'd miss a warm coat on a cold, windy day. Alva had been my comfort, but too tight of a fit. Using somebody as outerwear had to be wrong. My guilty conscience drove me to leave Alva. It was like having to see somebody you continued to cheat every single day, being confronted with the living proof of your wrongdoing. I'd look into those big, dumb, trusting eyes and say to him what he expected to hear, what he wanted to hear, but those words made me feel hollow. After a while, though the words rolled off my lips like stage talk in some long-running play, I'd grow smaller and the words swelled up with their falseness and I'd choke on them. That's when I started getting sad and Alva got that lost look and then he got mad because he said, "You're always going on about something. Think happy thoughts, go bowling."

I learned a great deal from Alva about one thing coming after another. "Of course you put the dish detergent in the pan before the water, it just works better that way." I'd ask why it worked better, and Alva would say, "Just because," and I'd shrug, run water into the pan then squirt the yellow lemon-scented detergent into the swirling water and think about being a guy peeing off a bridge. I did the opposite of what Alva said a lot of times just because I felt like it.

With Daddy nothing stayed the same, with Alva nothing changed. I liked that at first. I also liked the fact that Alva had a mother and that by our second date she had started to bug Alva about wanting to meet me.

"You'll love my mother, Chloe," Alva had said to me as he opened the door to his childhood home, a pewter gray frame two-story with vines climbing up the front of the house. Alva's mother was a tall woman with eyes like price scanners that went up and down you and totaled your value in under thirty seconds. I had worn a lavender dress and put a fresh coat of white polish on my flats. I wanted Alva's mother to like me. If she didn't like my dress, I was more than willing to take her fashion advice. By then we'd been going out for several months and Alva was pretty serious about me. I wondered whether I would be calling Mae "Mother." I wasn't sure I could get the word "Mother" past my lips, never having used it with any regularity with the exception of cursing, but I was willing to try.

Mae liked me, but not enough for me to marry Alva. She told Alva when I was in the bathroom, supposedly combing my hair but truthfully I was listening at the door, "It's a bad idea to marry a girl if you can't see her mother first. The apple doesn't fall far from the tree." That was very good advice, and I suppose now Alva regrets not listening to his mom. I should have listened to her advice too. Alva's dad lived a pretty much self-contained life in his Barca-Lounger with a path worn in the carpet to the kitchen on the left and the hall bathroom on the right.

But Alva wouldn't listen. He was in love with me. And I was in love with the idea of someone being in love with me. Alva brought me flowers and gifts, a silver chain with a heart that had ALVA LOVES CHLOE engraved on the back in letters so tiny you needed a magnifying glass to read them. I never asked Alva for anything, but I wanted those gifts. Sometimes I'd try telepathic communication to get Alva to buy something for me, like a stuffed dog with a dopey smile and long, soft ears that I rubbed over my upper lip. I got pretty good at that. I never wished for anything really expensive. I didn't get everything that I asked for. I wanted Alva to hug me more, and to kiss me without putting his tongue in there, but that didn't come natural to him. Lots of women could be happy with Alva, I'm sure of that. I just want things that he couldn't give me and maybe nobody can, but I don't like to think about that. I still have the necklace. I kept it just in case Alva turned out to be the only person in my life who loved me. I wanted to have something besides memory to prove I had been loved.

One night as Ethel sprawled out on her super-size recliner and I lay on the sofa staring up at the foam-sprayed white ceiling, she asked me, "How did Alva's mom take the marriage?"

"Pretty good unless you count the detective she sicced on me trying to dig up dirt."

"He find anything?" Ethel sounded hopeful.

"Not unless you count my father's brief prison record or my ten-month incarceration in the loony bin, hopeless cases ward."

"Really?" Ethel said it like "ree-lee."

"Nah." I didn't want to lie to Ethel. "Wasn't much to find out. No great crimes, no great deeds, just an edge-of-the-picture kind of life, mostly empty, a background kind of life."

She said, "My family had to do everything right. No white shoes after Labor Day, good clothes for church, a car that was new but not too new and not flashy. No putting on."

I told her, "At least you had a family. Three-quarters of the time, my father didn't know I was alive and the other quarter when he noticed me, I could have lived without the benefit of his attention. Mostly he noticed me when he needed something. I was like one of those pocket knives that does twenty thousand things like open beer bottles, peel grapefruit, skin bunnies, floss teeth, and act like a friend sitting in your pants."

Ethel stretched in the chair without making much movement, her weight barely shifting. "He didn't hit you, did he?"

"Not really, a smack now and then. Mostly he just ignored me. If we were walking, I'd have to walk real fast to keep up. He wouldn't wait for me. When I was a little kid, I ran all the time to keep up. Lots of things he didn't see, like one of his girlfriends used to pinch me. If I cried, she'd tell some story on me."

Ethel said, "I remember my mother slapping my hand when I reached for another sugar cookie from a plate stacked high with them. I think they were for her bridge group. I never liked sugar cookies after that."

"I've never liked sugar cookies." I drew out the "never."

"Chloe, you sure got a bad break in the parent department."

"It might have been worse," I said, secretly pleased at what she had said.

"Right, and being blind in both eyes is worse than being blind in one eye, but one will give you plenty of grief."

I started feeling pleasantly sorry for myself. I could probably start crying with a little encouragement.

Ethel asked, "You all right, Chloe?"

"Yeah, it's just that I cry so easy now."

"Well, any time you want to talk, my ears are open to your words. Not having anybody to talk to about what occupies your mind does you great harm. You don't want to start talking to food, the way I did when I was a kid." Ethel was now standing over me, her face a wide moon.

"You're awful nice to me, Ethel."

"You deserve all the good you can gather."

As I got up, Ethel gave me one of those big hugs of hers and I could have just melted right into her, adding another one hundred and forty pounds to her load, and just stayed there forever, part of Ethel, feeling safe. I could feel a smile on my face, not that curving of the mouth that kept people at a distance, that appeased them so they would stop talking at me, or about me or against me. Just a smile, a way out of my body, a way for me to see the world differently.

When I woke up the next day, the sun had already passed over to the other side of the house and shone full force into my room. On the kitchen table, Ethel had spelled out in M&M's TAKE THE DAY OFF. I ate the message one letter at a time, rolling each one around in my mouth, then crunching the shell and squishing the sweetness between my teeth. Everything tasted sweet to me today. I could probably drink vinegar and mistake it for soda pop. I picked up around the house singing "Simple Gifts." Alva had been wrong about me. I could be happy. I just couldn't be happy with him. Alva had thought that my life before him had ruined me, that he could save me, resurrect me. All he really wound up doing was burying me.

I could see it now how he had buried me. Telling me that I just thought too much about stuff. If I had only kept busier, say polishing that silverware his mother had given us as a wedding gift. The silverware that never came out of its velvet box except when Alva did his quarterly tarnish inspection. I often thought of marriage to Alva as a kind of a job, something I did to earn my kibble. A job where sleeping with the boss didn't violate any federal regulations, a job where I never had any time off. A stretch in prison where good behavior wouldn't shorten your sentence.

It's funny how you think that somebody's OK because all their sins are little ones and you're used to the home-run kind of sin, clear out of the park, no arguing, no hairsplitting, no questioning of how many angels can dance on the head of a pin. My daddy hit home runs: he drank, he neglected me, I was no more alive to him than a post. He went around me, behind me, sometimes he went right through me like I was a specter.

Much of that was my fault. I tried to be invisible. It made me feel better to think that he didn't see me because I had made myself invisible. That gave me a power that I know now I never really had. But then I used to believe that I was from another planet. That's how different I knew myself to be. I tried to hone my telepathic powers on cards turned face down, calling the card right before I'd flip it over. Sometimes I'd stand and try to pull all my energy into my forehead and wish that a million mothers would leave their children so that I wouldn't be the only one who didn't have a mother.

I considered not having a mother to be my most distinguishing characteristic. My father took better care of his cowboy boots that he wore to country-and-western bars to pick up women than he did of me. Just keeping me was enough to raise my father to sainthood in the eyes of some people. His girlfriends would alternate between gushing over me and sizing me up as to what kind of problem I was going to be. Sometimes they'd ask whether there wasn't some "woman family" that I'd be better off with.

Alva had always been interested in Daddy's girlfriends. He loved to lie in bed focusing on the smoke detector and listen to me describe the ones that I remembered.

"Chloe, tell me again about the one who took all your dad's money and ran off with the gas station attendant." Alva had come home from work, stuffed himself with spaghetti, and was needing to have some time passed before his very favorite show came on.

"Why do you like this story so much?" I'm sure I told Alva that story twenty times the first year we were together.

"It has movie-of-the-week potential." He started stroking my hair and I told that story again out of sheer gratitude for the way his hand felt on my head.

"He met Dixie in a bar. She was standing next to the jukebox singing along to some Tammy Wynette song. She wore a black leather skirt and one of those fringy cowgirl shirts. He told her, 'I like your voice. Let me buy you a drink.' They started drinking. He spilled bourbon on her leather skirt. She yelled 'you son of a bitch' at him. He kneeled down right in front of her and kissed the instep of her right foot. She had slipped out of her black pumps while they sat drinking. Having a man kiss her foot was a first for her. She said that she'd forgive him if he paid her dry cleaning bill. Leather had to be cleaned a special way. He gave her all the money in his pocket or so he said. It must have been enough. She came home with him that night and stayed for three months."

I really didn't want to tell that story again. But when I stopped, Alva's hand lay stiffly on the side of my head as if deciding the next move.

I'd start up again. "She called herself my mini-mom. I was about twelve. She's the one who told me how they had met."

"Why'd she stay around so long?"

"Because Daddy had a real good job pouring cement at a big construction site. She left the day after he picked up his last paycheck." Alva always asked the same questions. I always gave the same answers.

"How'd she dress?"

I glanced at the clock. I knew I wouldn't have to go through the whole story tonight. Only five minutes to show time. "She wore this skimpy underwear that was see-through and hung it all over the bathroom after she rinsed it in the sink." Alva had turned on the set and lost interest in the story. He moved away from me by a few inches and turned the volume up. I kept thinking about Dixie. I had felt embarrassed just to be in the same room with that flimsy stuff.

She'd let me polish her high heels and then she'd do my nails. She had a vanity case, pink leatherette with a clear plastic divider on top. In that she kept her nail polish, the bottles lined up by color: the pinks, the oranges, the mauves, the reds, the frosteds. Dixie felt any woman could wear any color if she just put her outfits together properly. I probably learned the little I know about fashion and beauty from Dixie.

After I polished her shoes, she'd let me sit with my hand in a bowl of warm sudsy water to soften my cuticles while I picked out any color polish I wanted. Dixie in her own way was a generous woman and I was sorry to see her go. She'd poke back my cuticles. I'd give an "ouch." She'd tell me that "women must suffer for beauty" and yank my hand back toward her to stab me again with the cuticle stick. Then she'd do my nails while she talked about whatever was on her mind with one sentence running into the next with "well."

I didn't mind not getting to say anything. She probably would tell Daddy on me anyway. I knew Daddy's women weren't for me. He wasn't looking for a mother for me. He just wanted someone to touch him in those ways that made him close his eyes and forget everything else. But I still pretended sometimes when I'd be out with Dixie or we'd all be out together at the drive-in that we were family. Daddy's girlfriends made my life better most of the time without trying. Having a woman calmed him, gave him something to put his mind on besides the rotten breaks he thought life had handed him.

Daddy never had any women like Ethel. He never looked at women who weren't skinny and who didn't own wardrobes about two sizes too small for them. I think he was a handsome man, but I don't think Ethel would have liked him even if she had been one-eighth of the woman she was now. But having Ethel would have been good for me. I regret that I can't remake my past. And I'm having trouble just seeing into my future.

All of Daddy's girlfriends were insincere. I could only judge them on their degree of insincerity. Loretta was probably the best and Carlotta the worst. Carlotta of the Spanish eyes and Latin temper who danced the Hot Pepper in every falling-down bar from here to everywhere. It was Carlotta who tried to put me in an orphanage and who kept asking Daddy if he was sure that I was his child.

I wasn't the only tumbleweed to land at Ethel's door. Ethel had a heart bigger than her butt and hardly a week went by without some charity case taking up space in Ethel's life and often in her house. The sofa we planted ourselves on every evening opened into a king bed. I didn't mind the stray cat who mistook my closet for an extra-large litter box, or the postcards sent to dying children who wanted to get their names in the *Guinness Book of World Records.* I recycled. I never referred to stay-at-home moms as not working. I was getting to be damn sensitive. I began to think that Alva ought to be here absorbing all this self-growth, not me. He was the chowderhead.

But Dean made me nervous. Ethel brought him home on a Tuesday night and he stayed for a week. He had these squinty little eyes. I went to the post office early on Wednesday expecting to find his picture posted with a description of his wrongdoing and I had hopes of a reward. No such luck.

"Chloe, Dean. Dean, Chloe." That was my introduction to a man who would be sleeping down the hall from us. I shook his hand. I could be polite. Dean acted normally but he was acting, I could tell.

"Ever done any acting, Dean?" I asked, hoping to flush him out.

"Not me." His eyes focused on me, an act of supreme will, I was sure.

He brought with him an old-fashioned satchel bag, the kind traveling salesmen used in the Old West. I studied the lock and thought about hairpins.

"Where you from?" I asked him innocently while passing the green-bean casserole. I expected him to say Sing Sing or the Iowa Institute of Incarceration for the Biochemically Disturbed.

"Nebraska."

I watched him lick up a dangling green bean from his lower lip. He didn't seem to notice that I was watching him. He worried me. I couldn't place him. He was like a floater dancing in my eyes, never landing, never still enough for me to take his exact measure.

"What do you do for a living?" I smiled brightly, a hostess smile. Ethel was looking at me but I ignored her.

"Won the lottery, had lots of friends, especially women. Then one day, the money was gone. The next day so was everyone except me."

I didn't feel sorry for him. My heart was stone hard toward him. He had been wasteful, foolish.

Ethel clucked in sympathy and passed him the sweet-potato pie. He ate a lot, almost as much as Ethel. She sat watching him eat and smiled. Ethel asked me to clear the table while she showed Dean the rest of the house. I used a paper towel when I picked up his plate and silverware. At no time did I come in physical contact with anything that he had touched. I must have used about half a roll of paper towels. I worked on, thinking that Ethel would appear at any moment and offer to empty out the trash or wipe the table. I could hear their voices—Ethel's soft, almost sensual, and Dean's short monotone replies. When I shut off the kitchen light, I found that Dean had taken my spot on the sofa. I sat in the extra chair, the guest chair, the outsider chair, the chair that should have been Dean's.

Dean and Ethel talked as if I wasn't in the room. Finally Ethel noticed my "negative vibes" as she would later call them. She asked, "What's the matter, honey, feeling left out?"

I could never admit to that. "Not at all. I was just wondering if Deano here has any outstanding warrants or maybe body parts in that satchel of his."

Ethel covered Dean's hand which he had placed disturbingly close to her thigh. "That is not very polite, Chloe. I didn't ask you a million questions, now did I? I have feelings about people, a sensitivity to their inner being. I felt good about you and I feel good about Dean. Now be nice." She interlaced her fingers into Dean's.

I had been scolded. I have always been good at maintaining my dignity no matter how tattered it becomes. "I'm sorry, Dean, no offense meant. Just a bit of humor." My voice dripped with Tupperware-lady sweetness.

"No offense taken. It's a might strange world out there."

"I'll be turning in now," I announced. A part of me hoped they would urge me to stay, that Ethel would urge me to stay. But she only called out, "Night-night, sweetie," her eyes on the television screen. Walking down the hall, I could hear Dean reading the lineup from the newspaper.

When I went to work the next morning, I took all my money, my identification, pictures, anything that might tell something about me. I put it all in a cloth shopping bag and wrapped giant rubber bands around the bag. It could fit under the seat of the van when I made deliveries. The rest of the time I would carry it with me.

At the shop, I could tell that Ethel wanted to say something to me, that she was waiting for just the right moment. I avoided her. I didn't ask what Dean was doing back at the house. I was fairly certain that he'd clean the place out before we returned. Then Ethel would be sorry, and next time she would listen to me. I was starting to think that maybe not being able to please her mother by being skinny had made Ethel want to please anyone and everyone.

Finally, right before closing time, Ethel blocked my way into the back of the shop. "What's the problem with you and Dean?"

I said, "He could be a killer, a rapist, a total depravo."

"He could be just down on his luck. Life's tough—like you don't know that." I'd heard that reasonable tone before.

"I don't trust him. He doesn't say much about his past."

Ethel said, "Neither do you."

"That's different." I couldn't believe she would put me and Dean in the same basket.

"He remind you of your daddy?" she asked.

My voice went up several octaves. "No!"

"Alva?"

"God, no." My voice dropped to a confessional hush.

"Then lay off." She said as if warning me off booze.

"Why is he staying?" I asked.

She answered, "I want him to. He won't be around for long. Just go with it."

"Maybe I should leave." I could feel my lip jutting out, a pout seizing up my face.

Ethel ignored what I had said. "Chloe, not everybody is evil. Some people just *are,* nothing else, they're just *there.*"

That made no sense to me, but I didn't argue.

Back at the house that evening, Dean sat reading a book on going into business for yourself. He had stacked his breakfast dishes in the sink. He looked up when we walked in, giving Ethel a thousand-watt smile and nodding in my direction. The line had been drawn. I was definitely getting into that satchel bag of his.

Dean entertained Ethel throughout dinner with stories of his boyhood in Nebraska, stories about cows falling into septic tanks, goats climbing into the back of the old Chevrolet and refusing to get out until they'd been given a ride around the farm. Ethel was a real sucker for animal stories. I studied the label on the salad dressing bottle and tried to memorize the spelling of all the chemicals they call ingredients. Dean complimented Ethel on her caftan, her cologne, and the Better Than Sex Chocolate Cake she had produced from the recesses of the freezer. The cake *was* awfully good.

Then, to my surprise, Dean actually cleaned up the kitchen while Ethel sat at the table telling him where everything went. I said I was taking a shower, and after starting the water I sneaked into the laundry room where Dean kept his bag.

It was a cheap lock. I had a pocket flashlight. I found exactly the following and nothing more: a small bottle of English Leather, three pair of pants, four shirts, a brown paper bag full of socks and underwear, two pens, a handful of change, and a wallet with a driver's license made out to Dean Snowell, age forty-three, weight one hundred and sixty-five pounds, height five feet eight inches, address some town in Nebraska that I'd never heard of, fifty bucks cash, and a grainy black-and-white picture of some old lady. No credit cards.

I jotted down the license number just in case the police had to get in touch with him someday. I had found out nothing that would help me get rid of Dean.

I tiptoed down the hall and had to take an icy shower, having run out of hot water while spying on Dean. I was totally awake. I heard Ethel and Dean say good-night, then Dean opened up the sofa bed. It cracked like an old man's bones when you pulled it out. The usual night noises, throats clearing, water running, spitting and rinsing, gargling. I just went along on that stream of sound trying to lull myself into sleep when I heard the squeaking.

The sighing sound that Ethel made sinking into her bed came

and went, but instead of silence, little notes of noise grew into a rhythm. I walked down the hall to Ethel's room. The door was ajar just the slightest bit, I'm sure it was. I gently pushed the door open another inch. Part of me knew what I was going to see, part of me was as shocked as a nun at an orgy. There was Dean, astride Ethel in all her naked glory.

He looked like a man on a mountain, a mountain of flesh. Dean looked pleased with himself. Ethel had this dreamy look and I knew then why she had let Dean stay. Ethel had a mound of pillows under her butt and when Dean got down to business I closed the door. I blushed, knowing that I had watched well past the point of shame. I backed down the hallway keeping an eye on the bedroom door, though I knew they wouldn't be coming out anytime soon.

Once back in bed, I tried to forget what I had seen, but my mind replayed it like an endless loop of film. I found myself reaching down to touch myself. Sex with Alva hadn't been much, but it had *been*. I did miss that. My body missed that release of tension. I was real tense now. I had traveled with my vibrator and an eight-pack of AA batteries. I had not used them yet. I needed them tonight.

I dreamed that night of mounds of mashed potatoes, serving spoon right in the middle, lakes of gravy, boats of hard rolls floating across the muddy surface, spears of asparagus launched skyward. But I didn't dream of Alva and I didn't dream of Dean and Ethel.

Next morning I expected to find the two lovebirds cooing in the kitchen but Dean was trimming the ocotillo out front and Ethel was posting bills when I came down to get a cup of coffee.

"Dean's offered to do some work around here. I made up a little list for him—guy stuff, you know. Any ideas?"

I read Ethel's list. Dean was going to be busy all day, but probably not too tired for a repeat performance tonight.

"I know what you and Dean did last night." I felt like I had shot a cannonball out of my chest.

Ethel stopped licking a stamp. "Pardon me?"

"I heard you two, you know, doing it."

"That bother you, Chloe?"

"A little," I said.

"Look, Chloe, most men won't look at me except to laugh and mock me. But I still have feelings in my body, I haven't buried them all in flesh, especially not the ones between my legs. They're the last to go, you know."

"What are you, a mercy fuck?"

Ethel's round face sagged and I knew that I had hurt her deeply.

"I'm sorry," I said. "I'm dirt. Poison's in me and sometimes it just comes out." I've never been sorrier than I was then.

"You got to start forgiving people, starting with your mama for leaving and your daddy for not being much of a man. I'm not out to hurt you. This thing with Dean doesn't have anything to do with us. Me and Dean need each other. He likes big women—some men do. Being alone is hard, you ought to know that."

Ethel was right but I hated sermons. "Look, I said I'm sorry, I didn't mean that mercy crack at all. I can tell he really likes you."

Ethel nodded, but I knew that unless I entered a time warp I had done damage here that probably could never be undone.

Dean left at the end of the week. Every night he and Ethel retired early. Since I already knew, they made no secret of what they were up to and their noises became louder. I would sit outside in a lawn chair with a jacket on and wait for Dean to come out into the kitchen to get an après-love-fest snack. When Dean left, Ethel slipped him a fifty-dollar bill and told him to write. He did, too— postcards, one a week, the first one arriving three days after he left.

I apologized to Ethel four more times, but I don't know if she ever forgave me. I realized that I didn't want Ethel to be mad at me, that having Ethel mad at me made me feel like something bad could happen to me at any time. It was as if I had lost my rabbit's foot, my beginner's luck, my fetish that kept evil spirits from my door.

I sometimes puzzled myself. Why had I been so angry about Dean? Once I figured him to be no serial murderer, I still didn't like him. Partly I didn't want to share Ethel, I knew that. But I had been so angry when I saw them in bed together. A woman had needs, I knew that. But Ethel wasn't just any woman, Ethel was like a mother to me—that thought gave me the creeps, made me feel babyish, a thumb-sucking weinerette. I was stronger than that. I gave up that mother shit years ago. I figured it must be time to move on. I was settling in here, sinking in, just like with Alva. Pretty soon I'd be neck deep in somebody else's life, a bit player in a daily docudrama.

I made dinner for Ethel and after cleaning up I told her that I needed to talk to her about something.

Ethel sat on the sofa in her usual spot, remote control in hand, two video cases next to her. It was movie night and Ethel had rented *Gone with the Wind.*

"I think I'll be moving on," I said.

"Chloe, why aren't you happy here? You're such good company. Zena might be back soon."

I hadn't thought about Zena in a while. I didn't think I wanted her to come back. "I've messed things up here. I've said ugly things and I've done things I'm ashamed of."

"Like what, honey?" Ethel rubbed her tongue over her teeth, a frown wearing a groove into her forehead.

"That mercy-fuck remark. And I watched you and Dean doing it, for a little while." I whispered that last half of my confession.

Ethel started laughing, the ripple starting at her first chin and traveling down her body until I swear even her toes were shaking. "So what? I knew you were looking. Hell, life's an education. You didn't peek nearly as long as I would have."

"What I said to you was cruel." I was certain of my own guilt.

"It was, but I know you were just jealous. Don't you think I see how much you want somebody to care for you?" Ethel tilted her head, her golden lantern earrings tinkling.

I was mortified. Stripped naked in the town square, walking through a department store in only a bra, a rawness I thought no-body could see out there in the open.

Ethel said, "I'm not going to hurt you, sugar. You stay as long as you like. I know you don't have any real ugliness in you, just stuff that others have left for you to sweep up."

I stood there, alternating between the red heat of exposure and the flash freeze of fear. Ethel patted the sofa. "Come on now, give me a hug and let's get started on this video, this *Gone with the Wind* is one damn long movie."

I sat next to Ethel, I hugged her, we watched the movie, and when Scarlett had hard times and Baby Bonnie died, I cried, but I wasn't only crying for Scarlett, Rhett, Bonnie, and the Old South. I was crying for me. This time for sure, I knew for whom I was crying.

Chapter Fourteen

My prayers were never answered, but the summer I turned thirteen and was fully costumed in a woman's body, everything changed for me.

All my hopes that something fantastic would happen never came true. I never found a stash of money that would allow me to leave Daddy to his women and his silence. I was never called out of class to meet the mother I only dreamed of, who would have an explanation for leaving me with Daddy all those years, an explanation that would make me forgive her and hate him even more.

I learned not to expect anything. At least that's what I told myself, but then I would betray myself and fill up with hope and desire—hope that things might change, that I could find the way to make things change, and desire that kept making me want things I knew I couldn't have. I told myself I didn't want anything. After all, I didn't need much, and I didn't have much. But in my heart I wanted everything. I was filled with such envy of others I felt sure my skin had a green tint of envy, the color of a 7UP bottle. At each new school I kept my circumstances mysterious, and with Daddy moving around so much, I constantly played to new audiences. After a while I started feeling like a stranger to myself, like I could be anybody and nobody at the same time.

Daddy started getting mail from the Florida Chamber of Commerce. He said it was time for him to retire, pick up a little part-time work down there, maybe painting work. Said he didn't want to work till he died, he wanted his bit of heaven while he still had a body to enjoy it. I looked through the brochures and thought Florida looked real good. I wanted to visit an alligator farm and stand on a white beach with foamy seawater swishing around my ankles.

I would be starting high school in the fall. We'd been in one spot for close to six months now, and I had known that Daddy would be moving on soon. He'd learned framing, but the house-building boom was slowing down and he wanted to go south. We started out a week after I graduated from grade school. I didn't know then that I wasn't going south with Daddy and wouldn't be having any sea foam swishing on my ankles.

Daddy bought me a suitcase, an act of generosity that made me suspicious. Then he told me to go buy some new clothes and handed me five twenties. By now the hairs on my neck should have been standing up, but dumbo me just thought maybe change had finally come, that all my patient waiting was being rewarded. I packed up my new clothes, my white underwear and my new bra with the lacy cups that a big-bosomed saleslady helped me pick out, and my jeans and shirts and one twirly skirt in a sky blue color. We were heading south all right, but only one of us was going the distance.

Along the way Daddy would stop at pay phones, covering the mouthpiece with his hand like I could lip-read and he had secrets to tell. He was in a good mood but he wasn't drinking. I went along thinking of seashells and wondering if the high school would keep the windows open and would I be able to smell the sea.

Daddy's mood seemed to improve with every mile he drove. I'd never seen him this happy without being on his way to a good drunk.

In a small town a long way from the ocean he stopped to gas up at a Mobil station. He stood there talking to the grease monkey who wore a brown coverall with oil streaks down the front. Daddy came out of there looking like a man with a mission. "Got a surprise for you, honey." I woke up then. Daddy never called me "honey." Half the time I didn't think he knew my name.

He turned right and then left down streets with trees arching overhead. It was mid-June, still cool in the morning. He pulled up in front of a small brick house set back from the road with round stepping-stones making a path to the house. Wait here, he told me, and he slammed the car door like some kind of announcement. A woman came to the door as if she'd been expecting him, maybe watching from behind one of those white curtains that fanned out from the open window like blowing snow.

They talked. She cupped her hands over her eyes to look at me. He handed her an envelope and then he turned, motioning me out of the car. I stood next to the front bumper, unsure of what to do next. He walked back to the car and unlocked the trunk, took out my suitcase, and put it down a few feet from the car.

"This here's a friend of mine, sister of a war buddy. You'll be staying with her while I get all settled in Florida." Then he waved good-bye to the woman who stood watching. Without looking at me, he opened the car door and slid in. He looked self-satisfied there behind the wheel, a man who'd accomplished something, the goal of a lifetime maybe. One more wave and he took off, dust rolling out from beneath his tires.

I picked up a rock, the biggest I could find. I pitched overhand using two hands. I missed. It thudded on the road, skipping twice. He didn't stop. I watched him drive off until I couldn't see the car anymore. I looked at the woman who stood rooted to the same spot in front of the house. "Come in for lunch," she called to me while holding open the screen door.

I picked up my suitcase and walked past her into a cool, dark kitchen. She snapped up a shade. "I keep it dark to keep it cool. I'll be doing a little canning later."

I put my suitcase down. "Wash your hands," she told me, and I did. She put a sandwich, a plum, and a glass of milk in front of me.

"Do you know who I am?" she asked.

"No," I said.

"I'm Dolly, your mother's sister."

There was a moment there when I let myself believe that she had said she was my mother. I just cut that word "sister" out completely. I couldn't look at her. I chewed the soft white bread with slices of baloney into gooey chunks and swallowed with small sips of milk.

I looked at her hands. They were small hands with scratches like tiny veins crisscrossing the roughened skin. I looked at her arms, the light hair glinting in the morning light. My eyes moved up the short sleeve shirt to her face. She had my eyes. She smiled. "How about a cupcake?" she asked. I nodded, the sandwich turning to starch balls in my stomach.

Slowly she told me everything, droplets of truth doled out through a summer of weeding, fertilizing, canning, and selling the surplus produce from a sagging booth with a neon orange sign announcing fresh fruit and vegetables. Mama was dead. She'd never be coming for me. She died the summer I was nine—hepatic fever, someday I'd look that up. This knowing sat upon me like a great weight.

"You look a lot like your mother. Except you got some wisdom on you. She never had that. She was young when she had you, even younger when the boy, Tom, was born."

I kept shelling peas and asked, "Where's Tom?"

"Adopted, I think."

"Lucy?"

She shrugged.

In the hottest part of summer when the heat becomes so heavy that nothing moves, when even bugs slow-motion their way through the humid air, I knew that Daddy was never coming back. I knew that the envelope he had handed Dolly had been full of one-dollar bills. I knew the money must be gone by now. Dolly signed me up for high school and taught me how to sew. By the time I entered the swinging oak doors of Centennial High School, I had asked all the questions I could think of and had all the answers I could bear to know. I no longer expected Mama to come for me one day, and I knew the symptoms of hepatic fever.

Chapter Fifteen

I had been with Ethel for about six months. She made no move to get rid of me and I made no effort to leave. With the free ride of rent and food, and a little walking-around money from Ethel, my cash was holding steady. I did my share around Ethel's, both at the flower shop and at the house, and I suppose I could have remained in what had become a damn comfortable life if Zena hadn't returned.

She returned the same way she had left. I opened the front door with a broom in my hand, prepared to sweep down the driveway. She laughed at my expression and said I looked like a fish flopping on a pier, a hook stuck in its mouth. I felt blown back like some tornadic wind had come through.

She hugged me, rubbing her cheek against mine. I dragged her suitcase into the house. It was hard-sided, the kind gorillas can stomp on and not make a dent.

"What's in the suitcase?" It was so heavy I thought the slightest touch might unsnap the latches.

Zena said, "Stuff, herbal remedies, books. I learned how to hypnotize people."

My guard went up. I didn't like anybody inside my head.

She grinned at me. "Not you, I already know what's with you. I'm just waiting for *you* to find out."

I felt like a box puzzle, all my pieces scattered about. I had thought about Zena coming back, but imagining didn't come close to the here and now. I wasn't happy to see Zena. I felt that I belonged here and she didn't. Six months had passed, two seasons, approximately one hundred and eighty days, without so much as a call from her.

"I know I didn't write or call much."

"You didn't call or write at all." I wasn't letting her get away with anything.

"I did too call. I talked to Ethel. You were never home."

Ethel had never said anything about Zena calling.

I figured that Zena was telling the truth. I shrugged and walked past her to sweep out the driveway. I wanted Zena to say something, that she had missed me, that she had a present for me. I wanted it so badly that I could hear her footsteps coming toward me on the asphalt. But when I looked up, the front door was closed and only the lazy cat that lived next door was looking at me, one yellow eye going straight and the other eye veering to the left.

After I had finished the driveway, I watered the flowers and picked off the spent petals. I put a petunia stem to my lips and sucked out the sweetness. I went inside where I drank two glasses of water and, between gulps, tried to listen to where Zena might be in the house. I walked down the corridor and saw that she was sleeping in what I thought of now as my room but at least she wasn't on my bed.

I went out to the kitchen to thaw something for dinner. I'd wait for Ethel to come home. Ethel would know what to do about Zena.

Ethel greeted Zena by hugging her tight. No questions were asked, no fill-in-the-blank statements offered, nothing except "welcome back."

After Zena came back, we held between us an uneasy truce. I slept in my own bed, but it was an uneasy sleep where the brush of my own hand against my face flashed me to wakefulness. I kept expecting Zena to hit on me again and I wasn't having any. I had pretty much settled that issue with myself. I knew what I needed and it wasn't to sleep with Zena again.

Zena disturbed the orbit of my world. I had created my own little habitat here like a gerbil nesting in a plastic globe. I had my little habit-trail and I didn't like the changes her coming back had made.

A competition was in progress and Ethel was the prize. It was amazing how many ways someone can work in the fact that she's a blood relation when she wants to. Suddenly there were stories awash in sentimentality and steeped in connection, stories about long lost relatives, closet cases, cousins related in some dim, primordial way to a famous general who fell on his sword upon learning the sad fate of the South. Over liver and onions one night, while spearing a gray slab of meat, Zena commented that she could definitely see herself in Ethel's baby pictures. The message was clear. I appeared to be an all-time loser in the relatives sweepstakes, starting with my Daddy, then Alva by law, and now this. Ethel tried to be even-handed, but those chromosomes sent out the call of commonality. I wasn't family.

But I continued to work in the flower shop and drive the van while Zena stayed home and threw the I Ching and gave tarot readings to the neighbor ladies for five bucks a pop. Most of what she told them came not from the cards but from peeping through the front windows and chatting up the neighbors, especially the old people who didn't miss a thing and loved the attention that Zena gave them. I recognized the technique. I was getting downright bitter about Zena.

"Let me read your tarot cards, Chloe."

"I don't believe in that stuff." I wrapped up the last piece of cherry pie. Ethel might want it later with some ice cream on top.

"You don't have to believe just to try it." Zena's hands moved around the oblong shape of the cards, lining up the corners.

Ethel called from the living room, "Go ahead, Chloe, let her. She did mine yesterday and something already came true."

"It did not." I was not about to believe that. Maybe I'd eat that last slice of pie myself.

"Yes, I got a very good reading with the ten of pentacles card, and yesterday that new Chinese restaurant called in an order for twenty-five mini-mums. Those people usually use plastic flowers, you know."

By way of agreeing, I sat down at the kitchen table and laid my palms out flat.

"I'm not going to read your palm, I'm going to do your cards," Zena said. She sat across from me and began shuffling the cards, then she handed them to me so that I could shuffle. "What questions do you have?"

"None."

"How about health, your love life or lack thereof, future successes, your job future . . . you pick."

"You pick." I wasn't giving her any help.

"Your love life."

I shrugged. I watched her lay out the cards.

"I see big changes in your love life coming right up. There's the Five of Cups upright. You're missing Alva."

"Right." I scratched my wrist and watched the white lines form.

"And I see the Lovers but they're reversed. That means dishonesty in relationships." I could see a smirk on her face when she said that.

I stood up. "You're full of crap, Zena."

"Maybe I am, but the cards never lie." She returned the cards to the deck. "Want me to read your palm?"

"I'd rather have my nails ripped off."

In her Lady Bountiful voice, she said, "Try some of that Tension Tamer tea, you're wound tighter than the inside of a golf ball. Stay away from coffee."

"Zena, thank you for the advice." Sarcasm coated my voice like a hard frost in late fall. I picked up the tarot cards and scattered them across the table.

"Girls, don't start fighting. This house is big enough for all three of us." That was Ethel's first acknowledgment that there was trouble between me and Zena.

Zena gathered in the tarot cards the same way she brought home a full house. She thought she had won this one.

•

If Zena made dinner, I'd make the dessert.

If Zena pulled the ottoman over by Ethel when we all sat watching television, then I'd bring the afghan over to her.

If Zena brought Ethel iced tea, I'd ask if she needed more sugar.

Zena told amusing stories about her time in New York. I told lies about places I'd never been but had read about in books.

If Zena praised Ethel's cooking, I'd compliment Ethel on her hair color which had progressed since my arrival to a deeper shade of red than nature had given her.

This went on every day, seemingly all day, spreading like some rapacious weed.

We started sitting out on the patio at night, the smell of orange blossoms in the air. A pitcher of margaritas sat on the table. "Zena, you thinking about going back to New York?" I licked the salt off my glass.

She said, "I might."

"New York's a good place for you. Lots to do. You've got a lot of energy."

"I'd miss my Auntie Ethel."

In a very polite voice I told her, "Don't worry about us. Ethel and I are like two peas in a pod."

"Family's important, but I guess that might be a hard thing for you to understand, not having much of one." Zena poured herself the last of the margaritas.

"Zena, from what Ethel has told me, they aren't handing any prizes out to your family."

"Meow, meow." Zena could do that. Cut right down to the nub of it with some animal noise. I had a certain respect for her, but I wanted her to get the hell out. I had something here that I'd always wanted, not the real thing of course, but a reasonable facsimile. I felt like I had a home and the closest thing to a mother I was ever likely to have. Zena had Ethel to herself when she was a child and now I wanted Ethel—and I didn't want to share. These thoughts made me feel peevish, like I needed a nap. I fell silent. I looked up to the sky, searching for the first star of the night so that I might wish for Zena to disappear.

A few nights later we're watching *Double Indemnity,* a spring storm swelling the streets with water, when Zena offers up that I ought to go back and see Alva to straighten things out. You know, make a clean break of it. She says maybe I should get back together with him. He seemed a fine enough man to her. Fine indeed, I said, I give him to you—no need to thank me. She told me how the movie ended, just to be spiteful.

We were like two piles of wood getting dryer and dryer, our words like matches flipped off thumbnails, flaming and then sputtering. And all around us the danger of fire grew higher and higher.

Then one night Ethel announced that Alva had called. Someone had given him the number at the house. I knew who had.

"Zena," I screamed, and she came out of the bedroom like a private called to attention by his sergeant.

"You gave Alva this number." I said this as a statement of fact.

"I'm only trying to help you out. You can't stay here forever, you know." Zena came down hard on the "you know."

I came back with, "You don't know half of what you think you know."

"You can't stay here forever," she repeated.

"That's not for you to decide." I glanced meaningfully at Ethel.

Zena drawled, "I've been told that picking up strays could lead to trouble."

"I'm not a stray."

Zena hauled out the big guns. "Your mother cut you loose."

"And your mother preferred any number of men to you." I was out for blood.

Ethel tried to push herself up from the chair, calling out, "Now, girls." She was too late. Zena and I launched ourselves at each other like heat-seeking missiles. I could have been clawing at anybody and at everybody who'd ever said or done a mean thing to me. I wanted to hurt Zena. I wanted to feel her blood like slime on my fingers. I wanted to scratch my mark on her, scarring her face so she'd never forget me. I wanted to punch her so hard and so deep that I'd know I had kicked a kidney or lacerated a liver. I wanted to leave marks on her that would last beyond death. I wanted someone to know I had been here. I wanted someone to bear the mark of my having been here, on this earth, in this body. I was tired of drifting, coping, getting by, making up stories.

Every punch I landed on Zena, every kick that contacted felt good to me, like poison being sucked out of my body. I felt as pure as a virgin. For every blow that Zena got in—and she was a good fighter—I'd feel pain for a few seconds, then nothing mattered except getting to hit her again. I wanted to empty out my entire body, siphon everything out until just a bag of skin was left with my skeleton jostling around inside. Then I could start over, truly be born again, no past, only my future stretching out before me like clean white paper or uncrayoned pictures in a coloring book. But this time, I'd get to do the writing, I'd get to do the coloring. Things would be the way I wanted them, not the way others had filled in the lines for me.

Ethel put an end to the fight. She sat on both of us, one butt cheek on each of us. I just lay there feeling all that fat hanging over either side of my right leg. My left leg was free, but I was beyond moving. Zena started yelling that she couldn't feel the circulation in her arm anymore. Then Ethel rolled off both of us. "Help me up," she said.

On the floor like that, Ethel was a beached whale. I favored leaving her there. Zena stood up rubbing the blood back into her arm. "Come on, help me get her up."

We hauled Ethel up, pulling her backwards onto the sofa. Her face had reddened and her caftan had hiked up to midthigh. I turned away. Everything seemed personal all of a sudden.

"Zena, you apologize to Chloe, you had no business talking the way you did."

Zena stuck out her hand. "I'm sorry, I really am. Forgive and forget, OK? Stay here as long as you want."

I stared at Zena's hand, my clenched fists at my side. I still wanted to pound her good.

Ethel stood, hands on her hips, her face fading back to her normal color. "And Chloe, you know Zena's right. You're welcome to stay here as long as you want, but you've got to do something about Alva. I don't want him coming in here like some oversexed bison full of heat, looking for you."

"I'll leave in the morning," I said.

"You can't run away from everything, Chloe, though you've seen lots of those who have. You're better than that. Decide things with Alva, make something new for yourself. You need to put down your own roots." Ethel took a deep breath. "And you need some ice. That's a nice shiner you got there."

I walked away, away from the ice, from Zena, and from Ethel.

I went into the bedroom, locking the door behind me so Ethel couldn't talk at me anymore. I pulled down the venetian blind and sat on my bed in the dark room. I watched the occasional car swipe the blinds with light as it passed down the street.

I had problems. I couldn't stay here. Zena had turned on me and so had Ethel. I was sick of their advice. Why couldn't they just say what they meant: Chloe, get out. Beat it. Your welcome has run cold. Move on because we have. I knew the message. I'd heard it all my life in one way or another. I don't know why I kept thinking that someday things would be different, that I'd find my place, like having some old family homestead willed to me. A place where I'd always be comfortable and I could do the keeping-in or the tossing-out.

Zena knocked on my door, said she had to talk to me. I ignored her. I heard her tramping around outside my window, probably checking to see that I hadn't climbed out. Ethel came to the door. She was mixing up some triple fudge brownies, chunks of chocolate in the brownie and frosting on top with sprinkles. Did I want some? I ignored her. I was good at ignoring people.

I should have gotten up and packed, but I lay on the bed instead, fingering the little embroidery swirls on the hem of the top sheet. I'd miss this bed, the way I would center my body equidistant from each side and fall into a deep, restful sleep. I'd miss the way the sun slanted in through the edges of the blinds, casting a yellow box on the wall opposite.

I didn't want to leave. I wanted to stay here. I wanted Zena to leave. I wanted Ethel to love me best. I wanted Alva to forget about me. I wanted to trade in my past for a future of my own making. I figured everyone's life has at least thirty-two percent sorrow in it. At least. Some of us get our sorrow up front, some of us get hit in midlife, some of us slip on the icy patch when we're old and on the way out. A few of us manage to make everyone we come into contact with miserable. Those people probably go straight to hell and collect their thirty-two percent on the eternity plan. When was I going to get my percentage of happiness which I approximated at fifty-three percent, the remaining fifteen percent being just boredom?

Everything quieted. Doors opened and closed. I listened as the house settled in for the night. The roof creaked as the temperature dropped a few degrees. After twenty minutes of only house sounds, I slipped out of bed. I opened my door and padded down the hall to the bathroom. I was on the potty taking a pee when I noticed the shower curtain bulged outward. I washed my hands, and when I turned around, Ethel pulled the curtain and there she was sitting on a kitchen chair, only a small portion of her actually touching the chair bottom. "I thought you'd never come out," she said.

"You look uncomfortable," I told her. I could smell the vinyl from the curtain and the stultifying odor of sweaty flesh and faded cologne.

"I am uncomfortable, but I didn't want you sneaking out on me. Women almost always pee before they leave the house."

"Ethel, I don't belong here." I was getting damn sick of saying that and sicker still of feeling it.

"Nobody actually belongs anywhere. We all just kind of land all over, some great cosmic die toss." She sounded like Zena.

"That's not right, Ethel. You belong here. You've fitted the house to you, to your size. You've taken what you are, a hell of a big woman, and you've made a world for yourself. I'm a stray, like Zena said."

"You are not a stray, Chloe, you're a beginner. You barely have the house plans for your life penciled in."

"I've got to move on."

"You got to know what you're looking for first. Just leaving something or someone is not enough. That way you keep looking over your shoulder. You need to look forward, ahead to the future. I spent most of my twenties and thirties wanting to be thin. I made a stranger out of myself. Then one day, I got so big there was no disguising it with A-lines or tent dresses. I just had to look at myself straight on and accept the fact that I was what I was. While I was trying out diets and sauna belts, my life was slipping away from me day by day because all I could think about was being thin."

"I don't want to stay with Alva," I insisted.

"I'm not saying you should. Only it seems pretty clear you're running from more than Alva. Alva's just a man, and by your accounting not much of one."

"Alva's just fine, thank you. I just wasn't the right one for him." I felt annoyed at Alva. Why was I always defending him?

"Maybe that's true, but what do you want, Chloe?"

"I don't know."

"Well, you can stay here if you want or you can leave. If you leave, you can come back. I'll be here like a convenient landing strip should the sunny skies turn dark and bumpy."

I could feel my eyes moistening up. No one had ever made such a generous offer to me. My heart swelled up with feeling and my chest felt so tight I thought I might be having a heart attack.

Before I could start crying, Ethel said, "Help me out of here before I start to grow mold."

I held Ethel's hand while she lugged first one foot and then the other out of the shower. We stood hip to hip in front of the bathroom mirror, Ethel in her flowered caftan, me in green tank top and jeans. I think I saw a family resemblance. I looked like an offshoot of a large multicolored flower, a bud ready to burst into color. Ethel still held my hand, and we looked into the mirror. We could have been having our picture taken. "If I'd started real early, you could have been my daughter," she said.

I smiled at the people in the mirror. I wasn't afraid of them. I'd go into a dark alley with them, I'd tell them my biggest secret, I'd let them see me cry.

Chapter Sixteen

One of the first things that I did after moving in with Dolly was to start entering contests. For the first time in my life, I had a permanent address. I was sure to be notified of winning. Dolly never gave me that things-are-going-to-change-any-second-now feeling. The woman was settled in her habits, her regularity a source of comfort to me. She never called me to account for the envelopes and stamps I used. I picked up entry forms everywhere. I trained my eyes to scan magazines and newspapers, counters and bulletin boards. I entered all kinds of contests, even those with prizes that I had no desire or possible use for: layettes, pots and pans, a free pair of eyeglasses. I just wanted to win. Each envelope I sent out felt like another inch in a climb up a pyramid of possibility, a bullet fired into my future. I could make things happen with a few words, a stamp, and an envelope. The mailman knew where to find me. I didn't win often, but when I did the sweetness stayed with me for weeks.

Besides entering contests, I also managed to learn the practical skills of canning, sewing, and making skillet dinners. I also learned that craziness surely ran in our family. No doubt about it—the crazy genes were there, encoded female. My maternal great-grandmother Sadie had been, by Dolly's account, driven mad by childbearing and the failure of those around her to share her vision. A woman before her time was what Dolly called her, a woman who generations later would have been called a genius, or generations earlier would have been burned at the stake as a witch.

Instead Sadie talked to those only she could see and together they thought women should vote and that there ought to be a limit to how many children a woman had to have. Why, she asked, was the sin of Adam visited so heavily upon women? Why, she asked, did a woman, who in most physical respects resembled a man, get treated like a draft animal, who only resembled a woman in the workload they both carried? Why did women need dowries? Why did incredibly ugly men think they could marry beautiful women—and do it? Her mind seemed to fall further back into itself with the birth of each child, eight in all. With the last one, she jumped from the hayloft in her ninth month. The baby survived being born a month early but Sadie broke both legs. That got her a few months of bed rest, and her husband, my great-grandfather, was advised to stop having relations with her. That hayloft leap was their last child, the child who grew up to be my grandmother. Dolly had stories about her too.

In fact Dolly was full of stories. I don't think that all of them were true, but I recognized the thread that knotted them together. I could see myself in my women relatives. Like the beaded curtains that fortune tellers use to separate their telling room from the rest of the house, I felt myself dangling along with my female others. I saw how their craziness flowed like an underground stream and then, when living tore up the protection of the earth, there it came—free-running craziness sluicing into daily life, sponging up the dryness, laying muddy tracks for everyone to see, and changing the direction of their lives forever.

My grandmother seemed to have it pretty well together until the change came and she started painting in the toolshed, using monochromatic colors and sitting nude on a three-legged stool. She had taken an ax and cut a hole in the roof of the toolshed to get the necessary light. By then the two girls she had borne, my mother and Dolly, had left home. Grandpa had retired from the railroad. He spent most of his time down at the tavern drinking the cheapest beer available and throwing darts, almost putting out the eyes of unsuspecting patrons coming out of the men's john. Grandma hung her paintings in the house and ran off for a while with some old guy who told her she had a "real feel" for art.

Before my mother died from hepatic fever, she had been well on her way to ruin. Like her grandmother, she had voices that came to her without benefit of radio or TV or even receptive fillings. She was a smart woman, Dolly told me. She liked to read the same as me but she just couldn't make connections. She tried to hold things together but kept finding life was like cotton candy—lacking substance, a disappointment, a treacly taste that didn't comfort beyond the first rush of sweetness. Mama kept after that sweetness, going through men until she had Tom, me, and the baby. Then she stayed with Daddy until she had to move on. Dolly kept telling me that Mama leaving me wasn't personal. That wasn't much comfort to me. It sure as hell felt personal.

Would she have been crazy if she didn't have kids? Is childlessness what kept Dolly odd but not crazy? Dolly was what you'd call eccentric. She always turned around three times in a circle before passing through the front door of her house. She planted rings of garlic to keep away evil spirits. She would often touch herself—first her forehead, then her collarbone, then each arm, then her belly, then each leg and then her feet—as if checking that she was all there and no part of her had flown off for a life of its own. Sometimes she would break into a sweat, stop whatever she was doing, close the house up, and lie down on the braided rug in the living room and shiver like winter had come on. I would put a blanket over her and try to talk to her, but she would hold her hand up to silence me and I would sit and watch her shiver until she fell into a deep sleep, drool forming at the edge of her mouth.

So though Dolly brought me no harm, she wasn't someone I could let go with, she wasn't really reliable. I worried anytime that things weren't exactly as they had been a thousand times before. I worried that Dolly was going nuts. She told me that most religions had a bite of the truth but none of them had the whole meal, and a

few weren't anywhere near the dining room. She said that whenever someone tells you that something is for your own good, look
around and see whose good is really being met. I learned things
from her.

Dolly stayed home whenever she could, which is what I think
saved her from the voices. She created this cozy little world for
herself where she felt safe—so that wherever she laid her hand, she
knew what she would touch. That sureness kept her from the craziness. Her death was what they called a merciful death, the heart
giving out before the disease could ravage the body and separate
sinew from spirit.

Dolly had left the house to the Humane Society to make up for
not caring much for animals, which she felt was her greatest character fault. A smarmy-looking lawyer whose mouth talked at you
while his eyes took inventory came around to offer his services. He
said I should contest the will but I didn't. I just packed my things
and took some pictures that Dolly had given me. I put them in a
small photo album: first my great-grandmother, next page my
grandmother, then Mama, then my graduation picture. When I
thumbed through the pages quickly, we became all one woman, so
that the last page which should have been blank appeared to have
someone whose picture hadn't yet been taken.

Chapter Seventeen

I woke up edgy, that doom-is-just-around-the-corner feeling settling around me like a shroud. Several days had passed since my fight with Zena. I still had a black eye but that was OK because her lip was still swollen. I wondered what Zena would do next. In some way, she'd try to tarnish me while glossing herself with a high sheen of righteousness, I was certain of it.

Ethel had left early for work, and Zena sat hunched over the computer in the sunroom where Ethel did her bookkeeping. I poured coffee from the percolator and sat in my robe at the crumb-covered table, watching Zena, trying to size her up by the hunch of her shoulders as she typed away.

"Zena, we have to talk."

Zena relaxed her shoulders and spun around in the chair. "We do."

"I know you're Ethel's niece and I know how much you love her. I'm not trying to take her away from you. I just need to stay someplace for a while until I find out what I need to do." My tone was conciliatory.

"I know. I understand. I brought you here. Sometimes my heart and head hit the same soft spot at the same time and, like a combining of the planetary orbits, trouble follows," she said.

"Let's be friends. No more fighting." I said it though I didn't really think it would happen.

Zena smiled, saying in an agreeable voice, "You're on."

I didn't know what else to say so I drank my coffee. Zena turned back to the computer screen and hunched her shoulders up again as if the act of typing required the shoulder blades to be bent.

I still had an unsettled feeling that no matter what the scoreboard said, the game was still in play.

I didn't have long to wait.

After a fast shower, I had dressed and was tying up my laces when the doorbell rang. I figured Zena would answer but the bell kept ringing. I stood up and walked down the hall wondering if it was the Jesus peddlers again trying to save my soul or somebody offering to trim the palm trees.

I opened the door and if Jesus himself had been there I couldn't have been any more shocked. There stood Alva, all two hundred pounds of him squared on his six-foot-four frame. He'd let his hair grow longer and the sun had flushed his face.

We stood there looking at each other. My mouth hung open. Alva smiled, his face filling up with happiness at seeing me. He should have been angry.

"How did you know?" My voice sounded to me like one of those computer-generated voices, remotely human.

"Some woman called me. Said you needed my help. Said you asked her to call me. You all right, Chloe?"

"I'm fine, Alva." I knew who had called him. Zena the little back-stabber.

"May I come in?" he asked, unsure of his welcome, his eyes searching my face.

I opened the door wider and Alva walked past me. I wanted to reach out and hug him. I wanted to take him back to my room and tear off his clothes. I wanted him to go away. "Too many things can't be changed, Alva, but I shouldn't have run out on you."

His words tumbled out: "I watch too much TV. I haven't even opened up the past week's *TV Guide*. Usually I just leave it on one channel and think about missing you."

I hated Zena. Here I was about to hurt Alva all over again. "It's not just TV, Alva."

"I know, my kids are brats. They just don't want to share me with anybody." He opened his hands in exasperation.

"Alva, I just can't stay with anybody now. I can hardly stay with myself. I only do stay with myself because I haven't figured out how to get out of my skin and move on, at least not in any meaningful way."

Alva lowered his head. I knew he didn't understand. "You're staying here?" he asked softly.

"I was coming back to see you, Alva. I *will* come back to see you. I was wrong to leave like that, just a note. Go home, Alva, and I'll come to see you. We'll talk, but I won't be staying, Alva. I just want you to understand why this is happening. It's not you, Alva—you're kind and you're good and none of your faults are above average—but all that moving around I did turned me upside down so that I don't have a compass anymore. I'm all confused as to my direction. I don't know where I'm headed, and I don't know what I'm looking for, but I know I need to keep moving. I married you to be safe, Alva, and that was wrong. I'm sorry, I really am. I burned bright like a candle and my flame brought you to me and kept you there when you should have been somewhere else."

Alva shifted from one foot to the other during my speech. I could see him struggling with the meaning of my words, trying to find some way to make things work out OK for him. I felt guilty, like I was a politician running for office, making promises that I knew I couldn't keep. But I was trying to be honest, I really was. I would go back to talk to Alva, but I wouldn't stay. I couldn't keep the real me around Alva. I had to hide out sometimes in dark corners, and his eyes were like giant lights sweeping the four corners of the prison yard.

"Things can change." Alva's hands rested against the pockets of his jeans.

Maybe going back and talking was a mistake. I could see Alva building a castle of hope from one little cast-off stone.

"I don't think so, Alva. I've been going over a lot of things since I left, and one thing I know is that I can't stay with you."

Alva flinched. "If you're that sure, Chloe, you don't have to come back. But I'll be there if you decide you want to."

I hugged him. I remembered his smell. My head fit just right under his chin.

"See you, Chloe."

I walked Alva to the front door. I wanted to keep parts of him and send the rest back to the ex-wife and the kids.

"You need money, Chloe?"

"I'm fine, Alva. Thanks."

"Who you staying here with?" He had stopped in the doorway, half in the house, half out of my life.

"A couple of women I met." I could see the relief on his face that I wasn't with a man.

"Chloe, you really coming back?"

"To talk."

"You might change your mind. Women are always changing their minds."

I couldn't push him out the door but I wanted to. "When you heading back, Alva?"

"Probably tomorrow. I saw a Holiday Inn on my way into town." He hesitated. "They're usually pretty nice places."

I knew he wanted me to tell him he could stay here. I remained silent. I slipped my arm into his and walked him outside, closing the door behind me. I gave him another hug. "I'll see you in a week, Alva, I swear."

He tacked an anemic smile on his face and gave me a so-long wave.

I went inside. I didn't want to watch him drive away, but I peeked through the curtains. I thought he'd taken things pretty well until I saw him push over the trash can left out for garbage pickup. Plastic bags and pizza boxes tumbled out. His rental car screeched around the corner and he was gone.

I ran through the house room by room, looking for Zena, but I couldn't find her. I decided to go to the flower shop and talk to

Ethel. I put Post-it notes up all over the house. They all said the same thing: "Zena: Thank you."

The flower shop smelled of coffee and dried flowers.

Ethel stood in front of the refrigerator case, moving vases around to achieve what she called "better visual appeal." I started talking before she had even turned around to face me. When I finished my tale of treachery, she simply said, "Sounds like vintage Zena."

"Alva's gone back home," I said.

"Think you'll ever find somebody?" Ethel sat ordering up the gift cards, her fat fingers pressing the right angles of each card into a uniform pile.

"No."

"You sure?" she asked.

"No."

"Well, if you do settle down, get married, whatever, I expect to be invited. I want to be there in some way besides memory. I'm too big of a woman to live only in memory."

"You could never be just a memory, Ethel." I liked that Ethel left open possibilities for me. She didn't run around slamming doors in front of me.

I walked over to the counter and straightened out the charge slips. I saw that the glass door of the cooler was covered with handprints. I reached for the Windex bottle under the counter and the roll of paper towels. Wiping off the glass, I wished that my life could be changed as easily as I restored clarity to the glass. Even knowing the genetic curse the females in my family lived under, I would never understand my mother. If life really did work out for the best—as some people claimed to believe, but which to me seemed another way of saying "God's will at work"—then Ethel would have been my mother, and my father would have been sterile. That would have been justice. But then I was old enough to know that justice was often just an idea. Heaven seemed to me an ultimate expression of justice while hell figured in under "payback is a bitch."

"You know, Chloe, you've got to make some kind of move here." Ethel spoke from her chair.

"Because of Zena?" I sprayed more Windex on the already sparkling glass.

"No, because of you."

I wadded up the damp paper towels, making the wastebasket with a left-handed toss.

"I told Alva that I'd come back to see him, to say good-bye the right way. Walking out was wrong. My mama walked out. I shouldn't have done that to Alva." It felt good having a plan.

"Then what? You said you weren't staying."

"I have about twelve hundred dollars."

"You could go back to school, stay with me. Zena will take off again soon, that child was born to stay rootless—but you, Chloe, I think you want to stick somewhere if you could get over being afraid."

"I don't know. You shrinking me now?" My voice sounded shrill to me.

"Just making suggestions. You think entering those contests is going to make things change for you? You must go through a book of stamps a week sending out those things."

I felt like my secret vice had been uncovered, like I was a guy dressing up in women's underwear or one of those people who sneak into closets and eat boxes of donuts, then claim never to be hungry. I guess I never really lost all hope. I kept entering contests believing in the possibility of my winning.

I defended myself. "Why not? Just like the lottery, somebody is going to win. Besides, I don't enter just any old contest. The ones with travel prizes and cash are the best. I'm selective. I just entered a contest to get you a new freezer. I do win sometimes. And I use recycled envelopes."

"When was the last time you won?" I didn't like the challenge in Ethel's voice, like I was going to learn something here whether I wanted to or not.

"I won some trading stamps when I was with Alva."

"What did you do with them?"

"I traded them in for cash and then went to a discount store and bought a yogurt maker, a Fry Baby, and a salad spinner. If I had traded in my stamps for stuff, I wouldn't have gotten the salad spinner."

Ethel shook her head like I was beyond hope.

Zena sat at the kitchen table fiddling with the tarot cards.

"Why did you do it, Zena?" I sat down across from her.

"I called him for your own good."

"I'm not talking about calling Alva." I watched her shuffle the cards.

"What, then? I'm psychic but I'm not a total mind reader." She wouldn't look at me. Instead she fanned out the cards, then swooped them up and shuffled again.

"Why'd you get in bed with me?"

Zena said nothing, but she stopped fiddling with the cards.

"Did you think I was gay?"

"Are you?" Zena asked, arching her eyebrows and looking right at me.

"I'm asking the questions here. Why'd you do it?" I stared at her and she stared at me, like two dogs having a showdown.

"I don't know. You wanted me to touch you, so I did."

"That didn't have to mean sex, Zena."

"You could have said no."

She was right. I could have said no. I had liked having Zena touch me, though I think I could have been just as happy to have her hold me. A woman's touch melted me, but I didn't think it was because of sex. I just wanted hands that cared—a woman's hands that cared, female hands that weren't my own. Hands like mine but not mine. I didn't want to be the only woman whose heart I knew. I wanted to be loved but I wanted to be free. Alva's love came with too many requirements. I wanted someone to love me just because I was me, not because I looked a certain way or could cook.

"I've done you a lot of good." Zena chewed on a callus on her index finger.

"You have, Zena. You speeded things up for me. You moved toward me while I was moving away. But the most important thing is that you brought me here to Ethel."

Zena stopped biting her nail. "It was all cosmically ordained, you know."

All I said was, "I'm sure," and Zena started laughing.

"Want me to do your cards again?"

I shook my head no. I stood up, sliding my chair behind me. I walked around the house gathering up the Post-it notes, which I stuffed into my pocket. I saw the mail truck go by across the street and I knew he'd be turning the corner and be coming right up our side. I went outside. It was late spring, and the desert was sliding into a summer of one-hundred-degree-plus weather. I'd heard stories of eggs frying on sidewalks. The sun hung in a cloudless sky and the air was sweet with promise.

By the time I reached the end of the driveway, the mailman dressed in his blue shorts and shirt and safari hat was holding the mail out to me. I said thanks and took the bundle inside. I waited for my eyes to adjust to the interior of the house, then I flipped through the mail. The usual electric bill, water bill, two magazines, one dating service flyer, four offers of easy credit, and an envelope from Standford Sweepstakes with my name on the envelope. I'd entered a record number of contests in the last several months as well as investing in the weekly lottery. I wasn't sure which contest the Standford Sweepstakes was. I left the mail on the side table and walked into the kitchen with my letter.

"What's that?" Zena asked, looking up from her cards.

"I'm not sure, a contest thing."

I opened the envelope after shaking down the letter so I wouldn't tear it. A giant koala holding the flag of Australia, a Union Jack in the upper left corner and a sprinkling of stars on a bed of blue, took up half the page. The bottom half of the page was typed, double-spaced. Zena leaned over to try to read my letter upside down.

We are happy to inform you, Chloe M. Herson, that you have won the Name the Koala Contest sponsored by the Australian

Tourist Commission. Your winning entry has won for you two round-trip tickets to Australia and a cash payment of five thousand dollars. In return, we ask you to appear in Sydney, New South Wales, one day during your trip for photographs and an interview. You will also be expected to appear at the Taronga Zoological Park to visit the koala whom you have named, Karaboo the Koala.

Please contact us at the number below to confirm your availability. If we do not hear from you within two weeks, the runner-up will be offered this prize.

We look forward to meeting you.

Sincerely yours,

Bob Wilson, President
Standford Sweepstakes

"Wow," breathed Zena. "Take me with you."

"No," I said.

"You taking Alva?"

I shook my head.

"Ethel?" she asked.

"I'm not taking anybody, just me." I folded the letter up and slipped it back into the envelope. "I've got a call to make." I could feel Zena's eyes on my back as I walked toward the front door. I picked up my bag from the floor next to the side table.

I think I heard Zena jumping up and down in frustration. It was a sweet sound.

I went down to the Central Library and maxed out my library card on books about Australia. I took out the Fodor Guide and even some kiddie books with mostly pictures. The ones I couldn't take out, I sat and read, taking notes in the spiral pad that I had started carrying lately to try to figure out my life. I'd been making lists: lists of things I've done, things I wanted to do, things I never wanted to do, my best qualities (I surprised myself by finding ten

of them), my worst qualities (my longest list), good things about
Alva, bad things about Alva (another long list), things I would do if
I won the lottery, things I would change about myself (I kept
scratching stuff off that list, which I took as a good sign). I had
taken up at least half of the spiral pad with my lists. Keeping those
lists made me feel I had more of a grip on my future. When my
thinking muddied, I'd make up a list or look up one I already had.

I went back home with my sack of books. I stretched out on the
hammock on the patio with my books stacked up next to me and
started reading. Zena brought me lemonade and dug up bookmarks
for me. She sat next to me in a chaise lounge, reading one of my
books. "You need anything, Chloe?"

"No."

"We had a lot of fun on that bus trip, didn't we?" Zena's voice
dragged me out of my book.

"We're even, Zena. I don't owe you, you don't owe me."

"I agree, we're in cosmic balance. But I'd really like to see Australia."

"No can do, Zena."

"Chloe, you know how I feel about you, don't you?" She offered me a plate of Oreos. I grabbed a cookie without looking up
from the chapter on the flora and fauna of Australia.

"I guess I'll just have to stay here with Auntie Ethel while you
travel the globe." Zena drew back as if she had thrown a knife at
me and was afraid the blood might spatter.

"You take good care of her."

Zena sighed and took a cookie. She gently rubbed my arm. I ignored her, though I had to reread the same paragraph five times before I understood it. Zena moved over to a lawn chair and let the
silence gel between us. I flipped to the chapter on Government in
Australia and memorized a list of Prime Ministers from Sir Ed-
mund Barton who took office in 1901 to Paul Keating in 1991.
Zena swung her foot back and forth, tapping against the patio table.
Finally she stood up and walked heavily into the house.

I felt powerful, almost like I could fly to Australia just by flap-
ping my arms. I'd wing my way across the sky like some giant

bird. On my list of favorite animals, I had picked birds and otters as animals I would like to be. The bird for soaring through the sky and the otter for being so free in the water.

I probably could have made Zena jump through hoops while holding out the possibility of Australia, but I wasn't like that. I thought about it, though, just for a moment or two.

When Ethel came back from shopping, I beat Zena to the front door by giving her an elbow and passing her in the living room. I told Ethel my big news with my arms spread out, holding Zena back. To Ethel's credit, she didn't ask to come along. She only wanted postcards and a baby 'roo if I could smuggle one back.

Chapter Eighteen

In high school I watched the other girls all the time. I didn't let them see that I was watching them. I saw myself as the audience while they were cast members. My aunt Dolly lived like a nun and boys made me nervous. I could smell them even if they weren't sweating. It was a sharp odor. It made me want to step back.

I studied the girls, all of them, the goody-goodies and the cheap ones. The goody-goodies had quiet hair that stayed close to their heads—grounding them—and they wore dresses with white collars. The cheap ones had ratted hair heading skyward and wore tight sweaters. The boys had more of a smell when they hung around the cheap girls. When they were with the good girls, all I could smell was their aftershave.

I hung back. I didn't mix much. I kept my back to the river of students between classes, twirling the combination on my locker, taking out a book that I didn't need. In class I sat in the middle, only raising my hand occasionally. I did my work but I learned more than I let on. I'd give the wrong answers on tests just so I'd only get a B. A-students got too much attention. At lunch I sat with the nerd girls. I was like moss on a rock: quiet, but a life-form nonetheless.

Being an outsider among outsiders wasn't easy. The nerd girls

had their own pecking order. Even Peggy, with acne and an over-
bite and a big butt, thought Evelyn, with her Mongolian eyes and
thick tongue, was stupid-looking. Fine distinctions were being
made. I didn't socialize with them, didn't even go to their pajama
parties where they all sat around hoping some boys would show
up, but none ever did of course. I just ate lunch with them and went
on my way. I think they let me stay around because I always had
my homework done and would let anyone copy. I already had the
knowledge in my head, I wasn't losing anything by letting them
copy. Maybe they'd learn something from my work.

Nobody bothered me because there was about me a certain re-
serve, an unknown quality. I couldn't be placed so, I was given
space. I was enough like the others to be allowed in, but not
enough like the others to be one of them. I zigged when everyone
else zagged.

Being an outsider suited me.

I read. Dolly would say an atom bomb could go off while I was
reading and I wouldn't notice. I entered those inked pages, passing
into a world so porous there was no longer any barrier between me
and the book.

I went to the movies and always sat in the fifteenth row, dead
center. I'd walk out after the show and hide in the bathroom, then
sneak back to see another show. An usher saw me one Saturday but
he didn't want to be bothered staying after his shift to turn me in.

I slipped up once.

But it was loneliness that did me in.

I had convinced myself that Dolly and all that space within the
contours of my mind and body were enough for me. I'd taste the
loneliness in my mouth first, a bitter taste like fear. If a sacrificial
altar had appeared before me, I would have laid down and arched
my throat to welcome the blade. More than anything, more than
safety, I wanted to feel not alone. I wanted to shelter myself from
the world with the bodies and hearts of others.

I knew my value. I knew my place card at the table of life. I
wasn't right up there where the food-laden dishes began their
rounds. My place was not at the foot of the table either, which

might be confused with the head of the table should the table turn one hundred and eighty degrees. My place was farther down, not the middle but past the middle, somewhere where I could see but I would not be seen. So when Sissy stopped by my lunch table to ask for my chemistry notes and I slid them out of my notebook and pushed them toward her, I didn't expect her to sit down and copy them right then and there. I expected her to flounce off to her own table near the exit where her friends gathered each lunch hour to comment on those passing.

She copied with a loose writing that stretched the first letter of each word up past where a capital letter should be. "By the way, Chloe, doing anything Saturday night?"

I looked at her. She had perfect skin, creamy white with just a touch of pink in the cheeks, and blue eyes that always looked widened in surprise. Sissy was popular. She had her own car, a blue Mustang.

"Earth to Chloe, come in. Doing anything Saturday night?"

I shook my head no.

"I'm having a little party, my place about eight o'clock. Keep it quiet, my parents are out of town. My cousin Ben is on his spring break. He's a college boy, you know. I think you two would really hit it off." She passed back my notes. "Well?"

I mumbled sure, why not, though I knew by the hair stiffening on the back of my neck that something about this wasn't right. Sissy smiled, waved, and walked back to her table, people parting before her like the Red Sea.

Evelyn of the Mongolian eyes and thick tongue leaned across the table and told me with her tuna fish breath, "She's up to something. Her cousin must be a real geekster."

Peggy put her face so close to mine that I could see unblended Clearasil on her angry acne. "Ignore Evelyn, she's jealous. Go, and dish the dirt to us on Monday. I bet most of those girls do it." Peggy held on to her virtue. She said it would be the greatest gift she could give her husband—her unblemished self. By then, she figured, her acne would have cleared up.

"I'll think about it," I said. I left them to buzz about my weekend plans.

Dolly made a fuss. She whipped through the clothes in my closet, making the hangers screech, then she went through them again. I told her it was no big deal, a totally casual kind of thing, but Dolly wasn't having any of that. She picked out a maroon dress for me to wear and gave me a dollar to get a new pair of nylons. She trimmed up my hair and made a facial out of cucumber puree and honey. I didn't know that Dolly knew anything about facials. I had never seen her wear nylons—mostly she wore serious cotton clothes, clothes to work in. She didn't go to church and I had only seen her wear a dress once, a long one practically to her ankles. She wore it to the funeral of her closest neighbor, the cat lady.

On Saturday night she dropped me off at Sissy's house. Dolly thought to ask, "Are her parents home?" I lied. "Call me if you need a ride home. I'll be up watching the Late Show."

I wrapped the strap to my purse around my fingers and waved good-bye to Dolly. Walking up the stone path to the front door, I could feel my dinner slamming against the walls of my stomach. I thought about turning back. But the front door opened and there stood Sissy smiling with all her teeth, holding a beer bottle and motioning me in. "Come on, the party's just starting."

It looked to me like the party had been going for some time. Kids sat on the steps leading to the second floor. Two lip-locked couples took up the sofa. On a wing chair a boy sat with a girl on his lap, his hands resting on her thighs, her arms around his neck. Several couples sat on the floor. I asked Sissy, "Where did all these people come from?"

"They drove. Parked their cars a few blocks away. Cars attract cops." Sissy handed me a beer. "So happy you could make my little soiree. Ben should be here soon. Make yourself comfortable."

I gripped my beer bottle and tipped back a mouthful of the yeasty taste. Sissy disappeared into the kitchen. I was the only person here not part of a couple. I felt like a social amputee. I made my way around the room, staying close to the walls, skirting the furniture, trying not to stare at the couples melding into one.

I wanted Ben to show up. I wanted to see what he looked like. Was he some four-eyed boy wonder with a pocket protector jammed with pens and a slide rule in his back pocket? I drank down half the bottle of beer. I could feel burning in my stomach, like I'd fed some kind of furnace, and I started feeling warm and loose.

Sissy came out of the kitchen again, arm in arm with some guy I had never seen before. She headed straight toward me. "Ben, Chloe. Chloe, Ben. Gotta go pick up Pete at work. I'm leaving you two in charge." Ben grabbed my hand and pulled me toward the stairs. We forced our way to the second floor, squeezing between couples on both sides of the steps. At the head of the stairs Ben sat down and pulled me next to him. I gave him a quick glance. He had dark hair cut short, and brown eyes. I figured him for about six inches taller than me.

I didn't know what to say. I could smell whiskey on his breath and he had a silly smile on his face. He wasn't bad looking and no pocket protector shielded his chest. He wore a blue striped seersucker shirt and dark pants. His aftershave had a woodsy smell. He kept my hand in his and yelled down for some beer. Two bottles began a journey up the stairs, passed one hand to another. I held the sweaty bottle in both hands and couldn't remember if I had finished the first one.

Ben started pulling on his beer. I asked him, "You in college?"

He nodded.

"Where do you go to school?"

"Florida State."

"What's your major?"

"Booze and broads," he quipped.

"No, really." I was about at the end of my social skills.

"I'm a business major." He rolled the beer bottle against his cheek. He seemed content to drink his beer, but he shifted his weight several times so that soon his leg was pressed up against mine. He finally asked, "How about you?"

"I'm a senior. I'll start going to community college in the fall. I'm thinking about being a vet." I hadn't told anybody that, not even Dolly.

"Why not a teacher, lots of women teach." He drained the last drops out of the bottle, then held my bottle up to my mouth like a baby bottle.

I finished my beer and he smiled at me and yelled down for more beer. He started the two empties on their return trip down the stairs. I wondered why I was here but I knew why. I wanted to see what this other world, always so closed to me, was like. I wanted to be on the inside for once even though I knew it couldn't end well.

A few minutes later Sissy blasted into the living room and turned on the stereo. Music jumped out. The kids started dancing. Pete, who had followed Sissy into the house, grabbed her in a tight clinch and began to baby-step her around the room.

Ben took my hand and I had no choice but to follow him down the steps. I felt like my eyes were off a little. I tripped on the next to last step and Ben caught me and his hands were familiar with the female body. We started to dance and I had to give him a little push away so that I could breathe. He whispered, "You're beautiful," right into my ear, and those words just passed straight into me like an IV dripping fluid and I swear I became lighter. I felt like a moonbeam on a clear night. I'd read *Seventeen* magazine. I'd heard this feeling described. I was in love.

Ben said, "Let's go outside for a while." In the backyard Japanese lanterns waved in the light breeze. The patio table and chairs were off to one side. We tripped over a few bodies as we worked our way toward the back gate. Ben mumbled, "Our spot."

"What'd you say?" First my eyes, now my hearing. Was this the effect of love?

"I said 'our spot.'" Ben's speech had developed a drawl. He pulled me down on the grass next to him. I thought about grass stains but not for long. "Sissy told me about you."

"What about me?" My hearing had suddenly improved. My whole body turned into an antenna, an early warning system.

"You know, you live with your aunt, she's a little different." He had his arm around me and was easing me back onto the ground.

I defended Dolly, "She's not that different."

"Sure, I know." He had me lying down next to him. "Look up at the stars."

I looked up. I could see the Big Dipper and the Little Dipper, the rest of the stars scattered like buckshot across the sky. I suddenly needed to find another constellation and know its name.

"She's different, though, your aunt." Ben's voice had a teasing persistence.

"She might be a little different," I conceded. I wanted him to like me.

"Some of the guys around here think she might be a dyke." He threw that out like he was fly fishing, a long cast and then the plunk.

I said as emphatically as I could, "I don't think so."

"But would you know if she was?" He had moved his hand so that it rested above my right breast. I was as conscious of his hand as if he held a knife.

"Of course I'd know. She doesn't have any women friends and she doesn't go out much. Why should you care?"

"If she isn't, do you think you might be?" His voice still had that soft, teasing tone. His right hand dropped several inches closer to my breast.

My early warning system kicked in. His hand no sooner made contact with my breast than I rolled over on top of him, my dress pulled above my knees and draped over each side of his chest. I had his throat in both my hands and I leaned down into his face. He clawed at my hands but I squeezed harder. "Try to throw me off and I'll gouge holes in your neck with my nails. What's going on here?"

He dropped his hands to his sides and I eased up on my grip. "It's just a dumb bet some guys had going. Your aunt's kind of an odd duck. People talk—one day you came out of nowhere, the two of you live alone—you know."

"What's the exact bet?" I sat heavily on his chest and stared down at him.

"I'm supposed to see how far I can get with you. I win ten bucks if I get inside your blouse, fifteen if I get inside your pants, twenty-five for anything else."

I asked, "How many guys in on this?"

"Most of them and some of the girls too, a lot of them. They're probably watching right now." He sounded hopeful.

I looked around. I didn't see anybody watching. Most of the

other couples in the yard seemed intent on merging into one. I tightened my knees around him. I leaned back down and kissed him hard while tightening my hold on his throat. He didn't know which way to go. He brought his hands up to touch my chest but I moved my knees onto his arms, gave him one last choke, then jumped off him. He looked small lying there, taking in breath. He squeaked out, "That was different."

I walked away. Straight out of that yard, through the house, right out the front door. I walked home, about three miles. It was midnight when I arrived home. Dolly was sitting up all expectant-like when I walked in. "How was the party?" she asked.

"A first, a real first, I won't be forgetting this one."

Dolly looked pleased and seemed not to notice that my dress had grass stains.

Chapter Nineteen

I walked up the sidewalk to what I had always thought of as Alva's house. He had taken the day off from work, we were going to talk. Tomorrow I would cash in the second airline ticket, and two days later I'd be winging my way to Koala Land. The sweepstakes company had expedited my visa and I was grateful as hell that I hadn't needed any shots. I planned on taking along my driver's license and high school diploma.

When I tried the door, the knob slipped in my sweaty hand. I wiped my hand on my shorts, gripped the knob again, and turned hard to the right. The door gave way and I fell forward into Alva's arms. I gave him a sisterly hug. I wanted to be absolutely clear about my intentions.

"The place looks good, Alva."

He smiled sheepishly. "I hired those cleaning ladies, you know the ones with the green uniforms that travel in groups of four and do your house in two hours."

"They do fine work, Alva." I looked around the place. Nothing had changed, everything was where I last remembered, maybe a little cleaner. Those women knew their work.

"Want a cup of coffee?" Alva headed toward the kitchen without waiting for a reply.

I followed him into the kitchen. While he brewed the coffee, I pulled two mugs from the cabinet. I thought about standing in Ethel's kitchen when Zena had taken me home with her. The sugar was on the second shelf like always and the half-and-half wedged between the skim milk and the orange juice on the top shelf of the refrigerator. I sat down across from Alva, wishing that the room were cooler. I was sweating and wanted to wipe my face, but I couldn't pry my hands loose from around my coffee mug.

"Alva."

"It was all my fault, Chloe. I just set like wet cement."

"Now Alva, don't do that. It was me. There's craziness in my family, all the way through, all the women."

"Mine too, what about my mother, you think she was all there?"

I laughed. "Mine were worse, much worse. Your mother was strictly bush-league crazy."

Alva gave me a tight little smile.

"Alva, I know this is hurting you. I don't hold anything against you. You can only be who you are, but I just can't live with that. Maybe it's me that I can't live with, I don't know."

"Chloe, I told you I could change."

I pushed away my coffee cup.

"If you changed, you wouldn't be you. You'd be masquerading, and all that pretending wears on you. Trust me, I've done it. You're you, Alva, and you ought to be enough. But it isn't enough for me and I'm sorry about that."

"There's no hope?" He had that puppy-dog look that made me feel like the guy who turns on the gas switch down at the dog pound.

"No hope."

His big hand reached across the table and covered mine lightly. I had never known Alva to be so light.

We sat there, his hand over mine, both of us looking down at the table. I studied the way his hand covered mine, only my fingertips visible. After a few minutes of looking, I felt like it wasn't my hand anymore but a sculpture in a museum, a piece cast in bronze, a part of art history destined for the eyes of strangers.

Alva lifted his hand off mine and reached back into one of the kitchen cabinets without getting up off his chair. He pulled out a box of powdered donuts—my personal favorite—and placed them on the kitchen table, a love offering.

My fingers scraped at the tearaway opening and fished out a donut. Alva took two. We sat in silence, eating donuts. I coughed on the white powder, then made myself eat slower. Eating in front of someone is an intimate act. I felt my lips press into the donut, my teeth tear into the sweetness. I watched Alva dunk his donut and then take a big bite. He ate three to my one.

"How long are you staying?" he asked.

"Just today. I'll leave tonight."

Watching the hope ebb out of someone is real hard. I wanted to make promises—promises to visit, promises to stay around, promises to be who he wanted me to be. I started to remember all the nice things that Alva had done for me over the years. How he had come out in a pouring rain to change a flat tire for me. How he always let me take first pick at whatever we had—pizza, pistachios, peanuts, you name it. When I had the flu, he brought home a case of Campbell's chicken noodle soup and an armful of tissue boxes.

If he had cried, I might have stayed.

But he didn't, he picked up the coffee mugs and put them in the sink. He balled up the paper napkins we had eaten our donuts on and stuffed them into an empty half-gallon milk carton he was using as a trash can. He used his shirtsleeve to wipe off the table. He said, "Let's sit out on the porch."

The porch faced east and was pleasantly cool. We sat on wicker chairs angled toward each other.

"Was I bad to you, Chloe?" Alva asked, his legs V-ed out in front of him as though he were ready to jump off the porch without any advance warning. He had all the ease of a jungle cat backed into a corner.

"Not really, Alva." I wished I had said I had to leave in a few hours. Alva needed to hear things over and over again. He was like a man at a funeral who couldn't believe the body was really dead, who marveled at the lifelike quality of the corpse, who couldn't accept his grief.

I wanted to make this easier for him, but I didn't know how. The one thing he wanted, I couldn't give him.

"We could make things work out," he said.

"I can't, Alva. I wish you'd stop asking me that."

"A guy's got to try, it's something guys have to do."

I changed the subject. "Need any buttons sewn on? Cellar need sweeping out again? Need any life-forms removed from the refrigerator?"

Alva laughed. I started to laugh and then reached out to hold his hands. "Be my friend, Alva," I asked him.

"Shit, women always say that. It's the kiss of death."

I laughed. He was right. "Have I done you great harm, Alva?"

Looking down at the floor, he said, "You've broken my heart. I just hope it mends stronger, like bones."

"That's damn near poetry, Alva. You're going to be OK." I tugged him out of his chair and pressed myself to him. It felt really good to have him hold me. But something was different this time. I didn't have that thin-ice, a-hair's-breadth-between-me-and-disaster sense that I often had. My feet were on ground that went down deep and never shuddered.

I took his hand and led him upstairs. He sat down on the bed and I climbed on top of him. I unbuttoned his shirt and he nuzzled my neck. We took our time. We both knew this one had to last a lifetime. I stayed on top and watched his face contort in orgasm and then relax into a smooth, almost childlike face. When I rolled off Alva to lie back on the sheet, I had tears in my eyes.

"You're going to be fine, Alva, trust me."

He laid his sweaty arm across my leg. "I do," he said.

Lying there, I thought about how easily I could slip back into a life with Alva. Passing through the house I had seen things I wanted to fix up. Those cleaning ladies were good but not spectacular. Cleaning ladies are like day care for your house. I could do a better job. But familiarity wasn't enough, nor was my feeling for Alva. Still I felt like taffy stretched out between staying and leaving.

"You got to go now, Chloe. I need for you to leave now," said Alva.

I had been running through a quick list of things that needed to be done in the bedroom. His remark jolted me back into the here and now. A breeze coming in from the window turned to a chill as the sweat dried on my body.

"How come, Alva?"

Because, he said, it'd be easier for him.

I turned onto my side, gave him a quick kiss, and said nothing about the tears glistening in his eyes. I pulled on my clothes and tied my shoes. I didn't look back. At the front door, I slipped on my backpack and straightened the picture of a fruit bowl that hung crooked in the hall. I thought about the tickets in my backpack. I had won the Name the Koala Contest and was going Down Under. It was the biggest thing I had ever won. I was going to the belly of the world and who knew what might happen after that?

I wouldn't be staying in a cheap motel, calling the truant officer on myself, entering contests where I never knew if I won or not because we'd moved and left no forwarding address. I probably couldn't enter any contests in Australia, probably they had a little line toward the end of the contest rules about being a citizen of Australia and all that. My visa would be good for three months. Maybe I'd learn sheep shearing, alligator wrestling, or kangaroo boxing. Who knew? I sure didn't, but I was on the move and that was what mattered.

I wasn't moving as my father had, drifting, rootless, always one step ahead of what he knew to always be at his back. And I wasn't running like my mother into the welcoming arms of another man, thinking that in touch I'd find my salvation. I knew that I had needed Alva. But although I'd be leaving without the armor he had afforded me, I wasn't the same person I had been. A sense of my life filled me as never before. I knew that there were certain things I'd never have, like Mama. But I knew too that the wideness of the world and the tincture of time would give me what I needed.

I'd come back. I'd find Alva a suitable wife, and I'd invent a mirror that would let Ethel see herself as I saw her. Lately I'd started looking in mirrors so many times a day that my reflection had begun to seem familiar to me. I didn't linger, didn't perform any checking-out-the-self rituals, but when I looked in the mirror now I saw someone, and that someone stayed the same whether I looked at myself six times a day or sixty: in all kinds of mirrors, in all kinds of light. I was there.